JM

m2

ROTHERHAM LIBRARY & INFORMATION SERVICE

R7G1

This book must be returned by the date specified at the time of issue as
the DATE DUE FOR RETURN.
The loan may be extended (personally, by post, telephone or online) for
a further period if the book is not required by another reader, by quoting
the above number / author / title.

Enquiries: 01709 336774

www.rotherham.gov.uk/libraries

"You really are a stickler for rules, huh?" Darcy said.

Before he could say anything, she added, "Children need room to grow, to flourish. Yes, they need schedules, but they also need to learn to be flexible."

Colin met and held her stare. There was no way this nanny was going to come in here and wreck everything just for the sake of making memories.

"I'll take her up for her nap," he told Darcy, picking up little Iris and heading to the nursery, Darcy following. With her little arms around his neck, his daughter still clutched the new doll Darcy had given her. Iris had taken to Darcy exactly how Colin wished his little girl would take to a new nanny.

Yet everything about Darcy hadn't measured up to anything he thought he'd be getting into.

Colin stepped into the pale green and pink nursery. A room fit for a princess...or duchess as the case might be.

He glanced at beautiful Darcy. The woman had no idea who he was...

And yet the pull between them was undeniable.

Somehow he'd have to resist his sexy new nanny.

What the Prince Wants

Wants

JULES BENNETT

MILLS
BOON
&
TM

First published in Great Britain 2015
by Mills & Boon, an imprint of Harlequin (UK) Limited,
Large Print edition 2015
Eton House, 18-24 Paradise Road,
Richmond, Surrey, TW9 1SR

© 2015 Jules Bennett

ISBN: 978-0-263-26039-7

Harlequin (UK) Limited's policy is to use papers that are natural, renewable and recyclable products and made from wood grown in sustainable forests. The logging and manufacturing processes conform to the legal environmental regulations of the country of origin.

Printed and bound in Great Britain
by CPI Antony Rowe, Chippenham, Wiltshire

JULES BENNETT

Award-winning author Jules Bennett is no stranger to romance—she met her husband when she was only fourteen. After dating through high school, the two married. He encouraged her to chase her dream of becoming an author. Jules has now published nearly thirty novels. She and her husband are living their own happily-ever-after while raising two girls. Jules loves to hear from readers through her website, julesbennett.com, her Facebook fan page or on Twitter.

To the Gems for Jules Street Team!
Thank you for the encouragement,
advice and most of all for the
support. I love you all!

One

The curves, the expressive green eyes, rich brown hair the color of his favorite scotch—all made for a punch of primal lust Mikos Colin Alexander hadn't experienced in years. This sure as hell was not the woman he'd expected to see on his doorstep.

Woman? No, she couldn't be more than twenty years old. She looked as if she'd just stepped out of a photo shoot for some popular American teen magazine. With her pink T-shirt, body-hugging jeans and little white sandals, this was not the image he'd had in mind when he'd gone online seeking a nanny.

Iris's angry cry drew his attention back to the

point of this meeting. The lady at his door immediately shifted her gaze from him to the child on his hip.

"Aww, it's okay, sweetheart." Her voice, so soft, so gentle, got Iris's attention. "What's a beautiful princess like you crying about?"

Princess. He cringed at the term, hating how dead-on this stranger was. But he was in LA now, not Galini Isle, a country so small that nobody here knew who he was. Which was just how he preferred it.

His wish to be free from his royal heritage had carried him through life, but the urge had never been stronger than after the accident that nearly took his life. Between that, his failed marriage, Karina's death and his being a widowed prince, the media was all over him. There wasn't a moment's peace back home and he needed to get away, to regroup…and maybe to never return.

Now more than ever he wanted independence—for him and his daughter.

"I'm sorry." Extending her hand, the lady offered him a wide, radiant smile. "I'm Darcy Cooper. You must be Mr. Alexander."

Darcy. The woman he'd emailed, the woman

he'd spoken to on the phone. The woman he'd all but hired sight unseen to be his live-in nanny because of her impressive references and the number of years the agency had been in business.

Na pari i eychi. Damn it.

What happened to the short, round, bun-wearing grandmother type he'd seen pictured on the website? He'd been assured the woman coming to care for his daughter was the owner. No way could this curvaceous beauty be in charge of Loving Hands Childcare Agency. Perhaps they'd sent someone else at the last minute.

Colin shifted his irate daughter to his good hip. Damn accident still had him fighting to get back to normal…whatever normal was after nearly dying and then losing your wife. "You're not what I expected."

Quirking a brow, she tipped her head as a smile spread across her face. Her eyes ran over him, no doubt taking in his running shorts, T-shirt and bedhead.

"That would make two of us."

Her sparkling eyes held his. Was she mocking him? Of course she was. She had no idea who she was speaking to…not that anybody here knew of his royal status, but still. Nobody mocked him except his brother.

Iris's piercing wails grew louder, more shrill in his ear. Between lack of sleep and the constant pain in his back and hip, he was done trying to be Father of the Year. The fact that he'd had no choice but to find assistance still angered him. Iris was the only reason he was giving in. Her needs had to come before his pride—which is why he now found himself staring down at the petite, yet very shapely, nanny.

This is what he'd wanted, right? To be free from all the servants, the media, the people ready to step in and practically raise his child for him while thrusting her into the limelight? Hell, he'd even been running his own vacuum here. Among other domestic tasks like dusting and putting the trash out at the end of the driveway. His brother would die laughing if he saw Mikos wielding a dust mop.

Colin. He had to keep thinking of himself as Colin now that he was in the United States. His middle name would help him blend in so much better. He was here to see who he was as a man, not a prince. To rediscover a piece of himself he was afraid he'd lost.

He just wanted these next six months to be free of all things involving his royal status. He was tired of being home where pity shrouded the faces of everyone he came in contact with. Yes, he was a widower, but so many people didn't know he and his wife had been separated for months before her death. They'd had to keep putting up a good front for the sake of their reputations.

Pretenses. That word pretty much summed him up. He wanted this freedom, wanted to see how he and Iris could live without being waited on hand and foot. He'd promised his brother, King Stefan, that he would only be in the United States for six months, the maximum time a member of the royal family could be away from the island for personal reasons. Then Colin would have to decide whether to renounce his title of Prince Mikos Colin Alexander of Galini Isle or return to the island and resume his royal duties.

Colin was first in line to take over the throne if something ever happened to his brother. If he gave up his position, the crown would be passed to their oldest cousin, who'd rather chase skirts and make scandalous headlines than run a country. That fact had guilt coursing through Colin every time he thought about the situation.

He'd temporarily lost his title when he'd married Karina because she had been divorced once. Their land had archaic rules, but that was one he hadn't been about to fight.

Now that his wife had passed on, he was thrust back into the royal limelight whether he wanted to be there or not. And with his daughter being the next generation of royalty, that automatically made her a duchess. The entire situation was a complicated mess. Added to that, he faced years of ramifications if he chose to walk away from his title.

Colin was determined to be a hands-on father. Being in a new country, still adjusting to this lifestyle and trying to cope with this damn inconvenient handicap forced him to admit he might need just a bit of help. This short-term arrangement would give him good insight into whether or not he could fully care for Iris on his own and if he and his baby should stay here.

When Iris arched her back, screaming as if

someone had taken her most prized possession, Darcy instantly reached for the girl.

Without asking, the woman swiped away Iris's tears and gently lifted her from his arms.

"Now, now," Darcy said, patting Iris's back and lightly bouncing his eighteen-month-old. "I'm not a fan of Monday mornings, either."

Colin crossed his arms over his chest as Darcy continued to speak in a calm, relaxing tone. Yeah, like that was going to work. Iris couldn't hear this woman for all the screaming. No way would Darcy's sweet, soft voice penetrate the power of a toddler's lungs.

Darcy stroked a finger across Iris's damp cheeks again. Little by little she started to calm as this virtual stranger kept talking in the same soothing tone, never raising her voice to be louder than Iris. Colin watched as his daughter stared at the stranger.

Within a minute or two, Iris had stopped fussing and was pulling Darcy's ponytail around. Strands of rich, silky hair instantly went to Iris's mouth as she sniffed, hiccupped and finally settled herself.

"Oh, no." He reached for the clump of hair that

was serving as Iris's pacifier, but Darcy shifted her body away.

"She's fine," Darcy assured him in the same delicate voice she'd used moments ago to get Iris under control. "Babies put everything in their mouths. I promise it's clean."

Colin watched as Iris gripped the strands in her tight fist and gave a swift yank. Darcy only laughed and reached up to pat the baby's pudgy little hand. "Not so hard, little one. That's attached."

Colin couldn't believe this. Iris had cried off and on all night—more on than off—and had been quite angry all morning. How the hell did this woman calm his child in the span of a few minutes? With a ponytail?

Darcy tapped a fingertip to Iris's nose before turning her attention to him. "May I come in?"

Feeling like a jerk for leaving her on his porch, Colin stepped back and opened the door wider. As Darcy passed by him, some fruity scent trailed her, tickling his nose in a teasing manner.

If he thought she looked good from the front, the view from behind was even more impressive. The woman knew how to wear a pair of jeans.

Perhaps she was older than he'd first thought, because only a woman would be this shapely, this comfortable with her body. He'd assumed all women in LA wanted that waiflike build, enhanced with silicone as the perfect accessory.

Darcy Cooper was anything but waiflike and her curves were all natural.

Colin gritted his teeth and took a mental step back. He needed to focus. The last thing he needed was to be visually sampling a potential nanny. He had to blame his wayward thoughts on sleep deprivation. Nothing else could explain this sudden onset of lust. His wife was the last woman he'd slept with and that was before his near-fatal rock climbing accident two years ago. Between the accident, the baby, the separation from his wife and then her death…yeah, sex hadn't been a priority in his life.

Years ago he'd been the Playboy Prince of Galini Isle and now his life revolved around diapers, baby dolls and trying to walk without this damn limp. Oh, and his glamorous life now included housework.

Yet a beautiful stranger had showed up in his house only moments ago and he was already experiencing a lustful tug. He wasn't sure if he should be elated by the fact he wasn't dead and actually had hormones still ready to stand up and take notice, or if he should be angry because sex was the last thing he had time for.

He and Darcy had agreed on the phone two days ago that today would be a mostly hands-on type of interview. It was important that Iris connect with her potential caregiver. However, he had nobody else lined up because there wasn't another agency that had measured up to this one.

Darcy had been here for all of five minutes. How the hell did he expect her to live here for six months if his attraction had already taken such control of his thoughts? His life was already a jumbled mess without a steamy affair to complicate things further.

Colin watched Darcy as she walked around the open-concept living area, bouncing the baby on one hip as if they'd known each other for some time. Iris started fussing a bit, but just like moments ago, Darcy patted her back and spoke in those hushed tones.

He'd never seen anything like this. He'd tried all damn night to calm his daughter.

Karina would've known what to do. Even though he and Karina had been separated for nearly a year before she died of a sudden aneurism, he still mourned the loss. The rock-climbing accident had changed him, had him pushing her away due to his stubborn pride and fear of not being the perfect husband and father, but a part of him would still always love her. She'd been a loyal wife and an amazing mother.

When Darcy bent over the sofa and picked up a stuffed lamb, Colin clenched his fists at how the denim pulled across her backside. Why couldn't he tear his eyes away? Why couldn't he concentrate on something other than her tempting shape? No, she couldn't stay.

What he needed was someone old enough to be his grandmother, with many years of experience, a woman with silver hair in a bun and ill-fitting clothing. What he did *not* need was a woman who could kick-start his libido without even trying. But, damn it, she'd calmed Iris and had done so with the ease of an expert.

"What is her daily routine?"

Colin blinked as he stared back at the woman

who was trying to be professional when his thoughts had been anything but.

"Routine?"

Dancing the lamb toward Iris's nose and then pulling it back, Darcy simply nodded without even looking at him. "Yes. Naps, eating schedule, bedtime."

Since coming to LA only days ago, he did what worked best for them and he was still adjusting. As hard as this change was, he wasn't sorry he'd made the move.

Colin glanced at Iris's smile, the prominent dimple in her cheek that matched his own. Sure, she'd smile for the stranger, but not for him? He loved his little girl with every bit of his soul. He'd give anything to be able to care for her on his own without the fear of his handicap harming her, but he had to face his own limitations to keep her safe.

"Mr. Alexander?"

Colin returned his gaze to Darcy who was actually staring at him. Oh, yeah, she'd asked him a question. Unfortunately, he was going to have to end this trial before it started. Having someone like Darcy here would be a colossal mistake.

Holding those bright green eyes with his, Colin took a deep breath and said, "I'm afraid I can't use your services."

Darcy swallowed her shock. What had he just said? The very survival of Loving Hands was contingent on her landing this job. She refused to take no for an answer. She couldn't afford to.

She also couldn't afford to keep making eye contact with Mr. Alexander's baby blues. No, *blue* wasn't the right word. What was the proper description for a set of eyes that were so mesmerizing they nearly made her forget all her troubles? The power he possessed when he held her gaze was unlike anything she'd ever experienced, so she kept her focus on the sweet little girl in her arms.

Holding onto a squirming Iris was difficult enough without the added impact of desire. Though she'd certainly take a dose of lust over the ache in her heart from holding such a precious child. She'd avoided working with babies for years, giving those jobs to her employees. Unfortunately, the entire staff of Loving Hands had been let go and Darcy had to face her demons head-on if she wanted to save her grandmother's company. So, his "no" wasn't an option.

This would be the first job caring for a young child she'd taken on since having been told at the age of twenty-one she couldn't have kids due to severe endometriosis. She could do this…she had to do this. No matter the heartache, Darcy had to pull through.

But first she had to convince Mr. Alexander she was the one for the job.

Turning to fully face the sexy father, Darcy kept her hold on Iris, who was nearly chewing the ear off the poor lamb. A sweet smell wafted up from the child's hair, no doubt from whatever shampoo her father used for her.

Darcy had learned from the emails and phone conversations that Mr. Alexander was a single father and new to the area. She also knew his wife had died suddenly just a few months ago. What she didn't know was what he did for a living or where he was from. The sexy, exotic accent that made her toes curl in her secondhand sandals clearly implied that he wasn't American.

Honestly she didn't care where he was from as long as he was here legally and the job posting was legit. He'd offered her a ridiculous sum to live here for the next six months and care for his daughter, and that money would help her save her grandmother's dying agency…the agency Darcy's ex had pilfered money from, nearly leaving Darcy on the street. Oh, wait, he *had* left her on the street.

Darcy didn't know what happened at the end of the six months, and with the amount of money he'd offered, she didn't need to know.

"You can't use me?" she asked, not ready to admit defeat. "Do you have another nanny service lined up?"

"No."

Shoulders back and chin up, Darcy used all of the courage she wished she possessed to cross the room. Closing the gap between them only made her heart pound even more. She would do whatever it took to pay tribute to the grandmother who'd given up everything to raise her.

Darcy's nerves had kicked into high gear before she'd even arrived here because so much was riding on this one job. Being turned away by the client hadn't been her biggest concern, either. Darcy had truly feared she'd take one look at the child and freeze…or worse, break down and start sobbing.

Yet here she was, holding it together and ready to fight for what her ex had stolen from her. Darcy had already given up her apartment and had slept in her car those first two nights until her best friend discovered what happened. Now Darcy found herself spending nights on the sofa in her bestie's overpriced, undersized studio apartment. This live-in nanny position would secure a roof over her head and a steady income to help get Loving Hands back up and running.

As if all of that weren't stressful enough, her would-be employer had opened his door and all coherent thoughts had completely left her mind. A handsome man holding a baby was sexy, no doubt about it. But this man with his disheveled hair and piercing eyes had epitomized sexy single dad. Those tanned muscles stretched his T-shirt in ways that should be illegal. Not to mention the flash of ink peeking from beneath his sleeve.

The man who all but had her knees trembling and her stomach in knots was trying to send her on her way. Not going to happen.

"So you have nobody else lined up," she repeated, praying she came across as professional and not pushy. "I'm here, your sweet little girl is much happier than when you answered the door, and you're ready to usher me back out."

When he continued to stare as if trying to somehow dissuade her, Darcy continued.

"May I ask why you're opting to not even give me a chance?"

His intriguing set of eyes roamed over her face, sending spears of tingles through her body just as powerfully as if he'd touched her. It was as though he was looking straight into her soul.

Iris squealed and smacked Darcy on the cheek with the wet, slobbery stuffed lamb's ear that had been in her mouth. Still, nothing could stop Darcy from trying to maintain some sort of control over this situation…if she'd ever had any to begin with. She had a feeling Mr. Alexander was a man who was used to being in charge. That thought alone had arousal hitting hard.

Focus, Darcy.

"Mr. Alexander?"

"Colin." That husky voice slid over her. "Call me Colin."

A thread of hope started working its way

through her. "That would imply I'll be here long enough to call you by your first name."

The muscle clenched in his jaw, the pulse in his neck seemed to be keeping that same frantic pace as hers.

Before he could comment, she kept going, more than ready to plead her case. "We discussed a trial period over the phone. Why don't we agree on a set time? That way if this arrangement doesn't work for either of us, we have a way out."

She'd care for Lucifer's kids to get the amount of money she and Colin had agreed upon.

"May I be honest?" he asked, taking a step back as if he'd just realized how close they were.

"Please."

Iris wiggled in Darcy's arms. Darcy set the toddler on the floor to play then straightened to see Colin's eyes still fixed on her.

"I wasn't expecting someone so young."

She was always mistaken for someone younger, which was normally a lovely compliment. "I turned thirty two weeks ago."

His eyes widened as he raked that gaze over her body once more. At one time she'd been self-conscious of her slightly fuller frame. Being surrounded by so much surgically enhanced beauty in Hollywood would wreak havoc with anybody's self-esteem.

She could still hear her grandmother's words on the subject: *Be proud of who you are, your body and your spirit. Nobody can make you feel inferior without you allowing it.* So Darcy had embraced her curves and her size twelve wardrobe, meager as it may be. Besides, who was in charge of dictating what was and wasn't socially acceptable?

Her ass of an ex had mentioned her weight. She should've known then he wasn't The One.

When Colin was done taking his visual journey, he rested his hands on his hips and shifted his stance. With a slight wince, he moved in the other direction. That was the second time she'd caught him moving as if he couldn't stand on one leg for too long.

"Are you okay?" she asked before she could stop herself.

"Fine," he bit off. "You don't look more than twenty-one."

With a smile, she shrugged. "It's hereditary and I'll take that as a compliment."

His eyes narrowed as he tilted his head. "It wasn't meant to be one."

Crossing her arms, Darcy glanced down just as Iris gripped Darcy's jeans and pulled herself up. The little girl with bouncy dark curls started toward the other side of the living area, which was immaculate.

Where were the toys? The random blanket or sippy cup? Other than that stuffed lamb, there were no signs a child even lived here. Even if they had moved in just a few days ago, wouldn't the place be littered with baby items?

Beyond that, from what she could see, the house was perfectly furnished, complete with fresh flowers on the entryway table and the large kitchen island she could see across the open floor plan.

"Perhaps you have an older, more experienced worker?"

The man was testing her patience. Withholding a sigh, Darcy focused her attention back on the sexy, albeit frustrating, guy. "I'm the only one available for the job at this time."

Not a lie. She was the only one—period. Just last month she'd had to lay off her final employee. Letting her grandmother's staff go had been heartbreaking, but the money simply hadn't been there after several of her clients had changed agencies. They had been like family and had all worked so well together. Fortunately, everyone understood Darcy's predicament and Darcy happily gave each of them glowing recommendations for other jobs. Hopefully she'd be able to get Loving Hands back on its feet and slowly bring her workers back.

"Listen," she told him, steeling herself against any worry or doubt. She wasn't going to borrow trouble yet. "I realize I look young. I understand how you only want the best for your daughter. However, everything I do will be monitored by you since I'd be staying here. You see something you don't like or you believe her care is not up to par, let me know. That's what the trial period is for."

Colin glanced from her to Iris, who was now smacking her hands on the coffee table as if playing the drums. Darcy wasn't about to give him a chance to answer, because she might not like the one he gave.

"I'm here now and from the dark circles under

your eyes, you need to rest." Darcy smiled, hoping he was not going to put up a fight. "I can take over while you take some time for yourself."

She waited a beat, her heart pounding. Would he send her away simply because she wasn't an old lady wearing an apron and sensible shoes?

Colin rubbed his eyes then raked a hand over his face, the stubble on his jaw bristling beneath his palm. Why was that sound so…erotic? His eyes settled on her again and she refused to look away, refused to step back or show any fear. This was her livelihood, her only option of getting out of the depths of hell she'd fallen into. Though being thrust into a lifestyle she'd dreamed about for years, a lifestyle that was completely impossible for her to have, was a whole other layer of hell.

When the silence stretched between them, hovering in the air like an unwelcome guest, Darcy was convinced he was going to show her the door. After what seemed like forever, Colin nodded.

"I'll give you today to prove yourself."

Two

Never before had he allowed someone to steamroll him into going against his instincts. Yet a determined woman with enough killer curves to fuel any man's fantasy for every lonely night had done just that.

Perhaps it had been her sensual body that had him caving and ignoring common sense. But Darcy had something else he admired—tenacity. She wasn't giving in and she made very valid points as to why he should keep her around.

Such as the fact that he would be monitoring her every move while she was here. Perfect, just what he needed. Watching her every move might very well be his undoing. He'd wanted to figure out who he was as a man while he was here in LA, but this unexpected lust was an angle he hadn't considered.

Colin clasped his hands behind his head and continued staring up at the vaulted ceiling in his master suite. Sunlight spilled in through the sliver of an opening in his blackout blinds. He hadn't even bothered getting beneath his navy duvet because he knew his mind simply wouldn't shut down, and getting too comfortable didn't really matter. Napping in the middle of the day really wasn't something he did, but he was exhausted.

Rest wouldn't be his friend for some time, he feared. He'd needed a nanny fast. Based on previous families his assistants had interviewed, Darcy was the best option. Unfortunately he hadn't had time to do a full background check on individual people, so he'd just placed a quick call to one of his assistants. Hopefully more information would come back within a few hours, but his gut said he could trust her.

When he told her she'd gotten the job, at least provisionally, she'd returned carrying one tattered old duffel bag. Didn't women have two bags just for makeup alone and another two for shoes? How the hell did she fit everything into one bag that looked as if it would fall apart if accidentally bumped the wrong way or dropped too hard onto the floor?

Before he'd come up to his room, Colin had offered to help her inside with her things, but she'd dismissed him. When she came in with so little, he'd assumed she had more in the car. She assured him she had it all under control and she only had the one bag. There was a story there, and if she was staying around he'd get to the bottom of it. Money was apparently an issue, so he'd be interested what her background check showed.

The cell on his nightstand vibrated. Glancing over he saw his brother's name lighting up the screen. Not what he needed right now.

With a grunt, he rolled to his side and reached for the device. "Yeah," he answered.

"I assume by your chipper greeting you're still on the nanny hunt and not resting?"

"I may have found someone," he replied, not adding that this someone would most likely keep him awake at night.

Stefan laughed. "As usual you're not going into

details. Fine. I figured you'd have given up by now and be ready to return home."

"I've only been gone a few days. I think you know I wouldn't give up on anything that soon."

Returning home only meant going back to the life of status he'd never wanted, raising his daughter in a setting that would consume her and stifle her growth. As the current duchess, she'd be in the spotlight at all times. He remembered how irritated he'd been growing up when he couldn't just go out and spend a day at the beach. He'd always been escorted by bodyguards, which seriously put a damper on his teen years and his ability to sneak out to have some alone time with friends—not that he didn't invent some pretty creative ways to lose the guards.

His parents had been wonderful, but still they'd had duties to fulfill, which often kept them away for weeks at a time. Then his mother had passed away from a tragic car accident and his father had been even busier, pouring himself into work and serving the people of the island in an attempt to fill the void.

Colin wanted to be there fully for his daughter. He wanted to form a bond that was so strong she would know just how much he loved her and that he would always put her needs first. Even before the crown. Which reminded him, his brother was still on the phone.

"I know you've never wanted this title," Stefan continued. "You do realize that no matter where you live, you're still a prince, but if I die and you've renounced the title, our cousin will assume the position? He's the last person Galini Isle deserves."

Why couldn't he just have a simple life? A life without the worry of an entire country on his shoulders? A small country, but still.

Again, it was times like this that he wished Karina were still alive. Colin knew his daughter needed a woman's guidance through life and he needed assistance with these major decisions.

"Listen, if an emergency arises, you know I wouldn't turn my back on you or Galini Isle. But I may have to renounce my title if I think that's the best decision for Iris." Colin sat up and swung his legs over the side of the bed. "Maybe I am making a mistake, but for now I need the distance. I need to figure out what the best plan is for Iris and for me. I'm all she has right now."

Stefan sighed. "If you came home, she'd have many people to love and care for her."

"I really need this time. Iris and I don't need to be surrounded by servants who look at us with pity. That's not what I want for myself or her."

"What about Victoria and me? We miss you guys."

Guilt had already eaten away at Colin's conscience, so Stefan adding another layer was pointless. He missed his brother, but they had their own schedules, their own lives. Years ago the two had been inseparable, often rock climbing or kayaking together. Stefan had stepped up when their father had passed from a heart attack and had scaled back his need for adrenaline rushes.

"When are you coming to the States for a visit?" Colin asked. "Isn't it time for Victoria to see her family?"

Colin's sister-in-law was from LA and was a member of the prestigious Dane family of Hollywood.

Stefan chuckled. "I knew you'd say that. Actually we're not coming for several months, but the annual royal celebration ball is in just over two months and we'd really like you here for that. No pressure, just throwing that out there."

Coming to his feet, Colin twisted from his waist in an attempt to loosen his back, which had wanted to tighten up and spasm a bit more lately. He'd slowed down on the therapy he was supposed to be doing at home. After this long he figured the prescribed exercises were a waste of time. Apparently not.

"I haven't even thought about the ball," Colin told his brother.

"The media will not be allowed inside the palace," Stefan assured him. "I can always smuggle you in via one of the underground entrances, just like when we were teens."

Colin laughed, remembering the numerous times they'd covered for each other so they could sneak out and meet up with their girlfriends at the time.

"Will you at least think about this?" Stefan asked. Colin knew he wasn't just referring to the ball. "Think about how hard life will be for you with no family and no one to help you with Iris."

Colin's mind flashed to the woman who had shown up earlier full of confidence and curves.

She was helping his daughter, no doubt. It was what she was doing to Colin that had him questioning his judgment.

"I've got everything under control," Colin assured him. "I need to go check on Iris."

He disconnected the call and slid the phone into the pocket of his shorts. Stefan had wanted Colin to think about this decision to leave the royal title behind, as if Colin had thought of anything else. The moment he'd discovered his wife was pregnant he'd done nothing but try to get out of that damn wheelchair in order to live for his child and be the sole supporter and provider—not in the monetary way, but in the fatherly bonding way.

Growing up with maids, butlers, personal assistants and even people who picked out your daily wardrobe was a bit ridiculous. Just because his family happened to be titled, because they had a certain last name and were wealthy, they had every single material thing at their disposal.

But money could only do so much. Colin still worried about the pressure and responsibility that came with being a member of the royal family. He knew he was projecting his fears onto his daughter, but he was her main source of stability now and he'd rather be overprotective than to pass along something that would overwhelm her.

Raking a hand through his hair, Colin opened his door and stepped out into the hallway. The twelve thousand square foot home was large, not as large as the palace by any means, but big enough that he'd had video monitors installed in most rooms so he could watch the feeds from his bedroom. He'd also had sound monitors wired throughout the house so he could hear Iris no matter where he was. There were alarms on the doors and windows, so he definitely would've heard had Darcy tried to take Iris from the house. He might be paranoid, but he would never take a chance with the safety of his child.

Colin was headed for the steps when his back started twitching.

Damn it. He gripped the railing as he stood on the landing and breathed deeply, waiting for the crippling pain to pass. Total agony he could tolerate, but being in a wheelchair and rendered helpless he could not.

Immediately following the accident, the doctors had indicated he might not ever be able to walk again, but the moment he'd heard those words he'd made it his mission to prove them wrong. Granted, he was walking, but the spasms in his back and piercing pain in his hip and down through his leg would blast him at the most inopportune times. Another reason he needed a nanny. Back home he had a driver, but he needed someone for that task here, too. Damn it, he hated being dependent on others for help, but he couldn't risk his daughter's safety if his pain hit while he was behind the wheel.

Colin needed to start making use of that home gym he'd had put in before arriving. He couldn't put off the physical therapy any longer, because he refused to be at the mercy of this injury.

Once the pain ceased, Colin headed down the steps carefully, in case the sensations returned.

Just as he reached the last step, squeals carried through the foyer. Colin followed the sound and stopped short when he spotted the carnage that used to be his spotless living room. He'd seen Darcy and Iris on the screen in his bedroom just before Stefan had called, but he sure as hell hadn't see this disaster.

"What the—"

Darcy sat on the floor surrounded by toys. Her

hair, which had been pulled back earlier, was now down and in complete disarray, as if her hands—or the hands of a lover—had been running through it. Dry cereal was strewn across his coffee table and had trickled down to the rug beneath. From the looks of things some of the pieces had been trampled on and ground into the carpeting. A sippy cup sat on its side, but, fortunately, no liquid appeared to puddle beneath due to the spill-proof lid. There was one blessing in this chaos.

While Darcy was smiling, her eyes on his, Iris was playing with the hair on a doll. Doll? That wasn't one of her dolls. Colin had only shipped her favorite things and this wasn't part of Iris's collection.

"Did we wake you?" Darcy asked, smiling as if this scene were absolutely normal. "We were trying to be quiet."

He'd turned the sound down in his bedroom, hoping sleep would come.

"You didn't wake me." He took a cautious step into the room, almost afraid to look for any more destruction. "Is this typically how you watch children? You let them destroy a house?"

Shoving her hair back, Darcy pulled a band from her wrist and secured the dark mass into a low, messy style. As she came to her feet, she wiped her hands on her pants.

"This is far from destroyed, Colin."

The second his name slid through her lips, his eyes locked onto that unpainted mouth. He'd been told numerous times how intimidating his stare could be, yet she hadn't blinked or even shied away from him. Granted, he didn't want to intimidate her, but he was pretty impressed by how strong she seemed to be. One more aspect of American women he found intriguing. So independent, so strong-willed. As if he needed another reason to be drawn to Darcy.

"Iris and I are playing, and when we're done we'll pick it up." Her arms crossed over her chest, sending the swell of her breasts up to the opening of her V-neck. "There were no toys in here at all so we quietly snuck to her room and I grabbed a few things. Then I wasn't sure what her eating schedule was and she was hungry. Took me a second to figure out what nack-nack was, but I figured it meant snacks when she tugged me toward the kitchen."

As she defended herself, Colin couldn't help but slide his gaze to the way the V of her shirt twisted toward one side, showcasing the swell of her breasts, all but mocking him. Then there was the way her rounded hips filled out her jeans in such a way that would make any man beg.

Prince Mikos Colin Alexander had never begged for anything in his life and he sure as hell wasn't about to start now because of some punch of lust to his gut that he couldn't get under control.

Darcy was quite a captivating woman. He still couldn't get over the fact she wore no jewelry or makeup whatsoever. The woman oozed simplicity and for some reason he found that to be utterly sexy and ridiculously arousing. She wasn't out to impress him in any way other than relating to the care of his daughter.

Iris squealed when she spotted him. With her little arms out wide, she ran across the hardwood, over the rug, crushing even more cereal pieces beneath her bare feet before she collided with his legs. Colin cringed when she reached for him. He wanted to scoop her up, but with his back just coming off a muscle seizure, he opted to take a seat in the closest armchair and pull her into his lap instead.

Iris's little hands smacked up and down his arm and he placed a kiss on top of her head, where her wayward curls always tickled his nose. The smile she offered him had him returning her five-toothed grin. How could he look at her and not smile instantly? She was his every reason for being, the motivation behind all decisions he made.

"How long will the living room be a war zone?" he asked, turning his attention back to Darcy.

She glanced around then back to him with a laugh. "You do realize you're raising a toddler, right? They will make messes, they will make memories and they will learn to clean up later. I assure you this area will be spotless once she lays down for a nap."

Iris wiggled right off his lap and headed toward the coffee table covered in a buffet of snacks. Weren't kids supposed to eat in high chairs? Had his assistants at the palace let Iris be so carefree when he hadn't been around?

"She's been playing in her room," Colin informed Darcy when she continued to stare at him. "That's why the toys are kept there."

A wide smile spread across Darcy's face, making her look even younger. "You really are a stickler for rules, huh? Children need room to grow, to flourish. Yes, they need schedules, but they also need to learn to be flexible."

Even though she stood above him, Colin met and held her stare. There was no way this nanny was going to come in here and wreck everything just for the sake of making memories or whatever the hell else she'd babbled about.

Colin wasn't stupid. He knew he owed his not-so-sunny disposition to the fact that he couldn't get a grip on his attraction. Why this woman? Why now? And why the hell were her breasts right at eye level?

"By flourish do you mean grinding cereal into the floor?" he asked, focusing on the mess. "Or maybe you mean throwing toys around the room without a care of what may break?"

"That was another point I was going to bring up." Darcy stepped over a stuffed animal and sank down on the edge of the sofa. Lacing her fingers over the arm, she brought her eyes back to his. "All of these breakables should probably be put away for now, or at least placed higher where she can't pull them down. She'll get used to what she can and can't touch, but for now I'd try to avoid unnecessary injuries."

The home had come fully furnished. Colin had simply paid a designer to get everything set up so he only had to bring their clothes and personal belongings. All the breakables and any other knickknacks sitting around meant nothing to him. He'd replace whatever was broken, if need be.

Colin glanced across the mayhem on the floor. Iris sat on her beloved lamb while playing with the new doll.

"Where did that come from?"

Darcy glanced over as Iris gripped the doll's long, dark hair and started swinging it around. "I brought it for her."

So in the single bag she'd brought, Darcy had managed to squeeze a doll in among her belongings?

"Is that something you normally do? Bribe potential clients?"

Darcy's eyes widened. "I've never had to bribe

anybody. Your daughter was being introduced to a stranger and I used the doll as a way to talk to her and make her comfortable. I can take it back if it offends you."

Colin gritted his teeth. In the span of a few hours his house had been taken over by this free spirit who seemed oblivious to the mess surrounding them and was trying to tell him how to raise his child. She'd calmed Iris in a way he'd never seen and now his new nanny was stomping all over his libido. And he was paying her for every bit of this torture.

Iris started whimpering as she rubbed her eyes.

"Is this nap time?" Darcy asked.

"She tends to nap once a day." He smoothed a wayward curl from Iris's forehead and slid his finger down her silky cheek. "There's no set time. I just lay her down when she seems ready."

Darcy came to her feet, crossed the room and lifted Iris into her arms. "Come on, sweetheart. Let's get you down for a nap. I'll clean the mess today and you can help tomorrow."

Colin rose. Now that he didn't have to bend over and pick Iris up, he figured he could carry her to her bedroom. He hadn't felt even a twinge in his back since he'd been downstairs.

"I'll take her up." Colin took Iris from Darcy's arms, careful not to brush against any part of her tempting body. "You can work on this."

Holding his daughter tight, he headed up to the nursery. With her little arms around his neck, she still clutched the new doll and with each step he took it slapped against his back. Iris had taken to Darcy exactly the way Colin hoped his little girl would take to a new nanny. Yet some things about Darcy didn't add up. He'd picked her agency because of its reputation and level of experience. Okay, so she was older than he'd first thought. But why did she have so few belongings and why were her clothes a bit on the cheap, hand-me-down side?

With Iris nuzzling his neck, Colin stepped into the pale green and pink nursery. This was the one room he'd had painted before they'd moved in. Every other room had just been furnished as he'd requested. He'd wanted something special for Iris and the designer really went all out with the round crib in the middle of the spacious room, sheer draping suspended from the ceiling that flowed down over the bed and classic white furniture complete with all things girly, pink and just a touch of sparkle. The floor-to-ceiling window also had sheer curtains that were tied back with some pink, shimmery material, and toy bins were stacked neatly against the far wall.

A room fit for a princess...or duchess, as the case may be.

When he sat Iris in her bed, she quickly grabbed her little heart pillow, hugged her new doll to her chest and lay down. Colin watched until her eyes closed, her breathing slowed.

Darcy might be a bit of a mystery, but with his status, he had to be extremely watchful. She seemed trustworthy so far. If she just wanted privacy that was one thing. Who was he to judge? Wasn't he lying and pretending to be someone else right now?

The fact that there was more to figure out with the alluring, frustrating nanny left him no choice but to head back downstairs and talk with her now that they were alone.

Of course, he was hiding the fact that he was a prince, one who found her to be sexy as hell. Still, he needed help with Iris. For now he'd have to keep Darcy around, but that didn't mean she'd be here for the full six months. They needed to pin down a suitable trial period. In the meantime, he could be researching a backup in case Darcy didn't work out.

Regardless of the end result, he had to ignore how enticing she was. Romance, whether short- or long-term, was not on his agenda, and he sure as hell wouldn't be so trite as to fall into bed with his baby's nanny.

Three

Darcy had picked up the living room, piling all the toys and infant blankets neatly in the corner. The rogue cereal pieces were in the trash, except for the crushed bits. She'd have to ask Colin where the vacuum was kept to get the rug back in order. She'd work with Iris and her cleaning skills next time. The girl needed a nap more than she needed a lesson.

Playing with Iris, truly feeling a bond starting to form, was both a blessing and an ache she couldn't begin to put into words. For so long she'd had that little-girl dream of having her own family, but such things were not meant to be. Darcy hadn't thought this job would be so intense, yet

maybe it was the combination of the baby and the
man that had her stomach in knots. As grouchy
as he was, Colin was still very sexy, there was
no denying the obvious.

At first, the instant attraction to Colin had lay-
ered over her anxiety of working with an infant.
The man was hot, hot, hot, and that was just the
physical packaging. When he spoke with that accent he only rose another notch on the sexy scale.
But there was nothing like seeing him holding
his beautiful daughter, the way he looked at her
with all the love in the world. Something about
watching him with his guard down had Darcy
melting even more.

As Colin's footsteps pounded down the steps,
she stood at the kitchen sink rinsing the sippy
cup. Quickly placing it on the drying mat, she
wiped her hands on her jeans. She had no clue
what mood Colin would be in or how he might
react once they were alone.

Would he ask her to leave simply because of the
mess? A good first impression was everything
and she'd probably blown it. He'd told her she had
until the end of the day to prove herself, but she
may not make it that far. She stood to lose her

pride and her grandmother's legacy. There was no plan B, there was no knight who would ride to her rescue. So if Colin was angry enough to ask her to go, she wouldn't have much choice.

Darcy couldn't get a good read on him. When he looked at her she couldn't tell if he was angry or turned on. Ridiculous to think a piece of eye candy like Colin Alexander would find her attractive, but he volleyed between being pissed and raking his eyes over her.

No way would she bring up the fact he turned her inside out. She'd always been a professional and this job was no different…except for the fact she needed this one more than any other.

Just as Darcy turned, Colin was rounding the large center island. Even in the openness of the kitchen, the man seemed to dominate the room. She stepped back, the edge of the counter biting into the small of her back.

"Is she asleep?" Darcy asked, trying to keep her voice steady, though she felt anything but.

"Yes." His eyes pinned her in place as he rested one hand on the granite counter. "We need to talk while she's down."

Swallowing, Darcy nodded. This was like the

equivalent of the breakup in a business setting. Still, she wouldn't go down without a fight.

"I need to clean the rug first," she told him, knowing he probably recognized the stalling tactic. "I wasn't sure where you kept your vacuum."

"There's a handheld one in the utility room. I'll get it later."

Oh, this wasn't good. An image of her grandmother flashed through her mind. Darcy had promised Gram before she passed that Loving Hands would stay up and running. Then love had entered the picture...or what Darcy had thought was love. How could she have been so naive as to trust a man with her life and her family business, and not see that he was a lying, greedy user?

Colin leaned against the island and crossed his arms over his broad chest. "Why only one bag?"

His question jerked her from her thoughts. That's what he'd initially wanted to talk about? Her luggage?

"How many bags do I need?" she countered.

A sliver of a tattoo peeked out from beneath the hem of his T-shirt sleeve. Darcy's belly clenched. She'd always been a sucker for ink. But shallow lust is what got her into a mess of trouble the last time. A sexy, smooth-talking man and tats over solid muscles…she refused to go down the same path again, when all she'd met at the end of her journey was a broken heart. Not that Colin was a smooth talker. He was more of a blunt, grumpy, irritable talker.

"Will you be sending for more belongings?" he asked.

Still stunned that this was what he'd wanted to discuss, she shook her head. "I have all I need. Does this mean I'm staying?"

When he raked a hand through his tousled hair, a masculine, woodsy scent slid across the gap and straight to her. How did the man positively reek of sex appeal when he looked like he'd spent days without sleep?

"I want to discuss the trial period," he told her, shifting his weight with a slight wince. "The contract we mentioned on the phone was for six months. I'll give you one month to prove that you're the right fit for the job. Anytime in that month we can decide to terminate the agreement."

Relief spread through her in waves. She would

definitely win him over in a month. She was good at her job, she'd been raised helping her grandmother care for children and, honestly, raising kids was all she knew. The irony of the situation as it related to her personal struggles was not lost on her.

And, actually, caring for kids wasn't all she knew, just all she knew to pay her bills. Cooking was her hobby, her therapy, really, but it wouldn't keep her afloat financially no matter how much she enjoyed it.

"That sounds fair." She rested her hands on either side of her hips, gripping the edge of the counter with her palms.

"I know we agreed on compensation," he went on as if conducting a business meeting and not standing in his kitchen with sexual tension vibrating between them. "I'll give you half now and the other half at the end of the six months, if you stay. Between now and the sixth month, there may be incentives along the way. Bonuses, if you will."

"And if I leave at the end of this month?"

Colin's bright eyes held hers as he lifted a

shoulder. "Then take the first half of the money and go. No incentives."

Half the money was better than no money. Still, she needed the full amount to pay off Thad's debt and jumpstart the agency again. This job would save her business and get her back where she needed to be so she would make sure she impressed him with her skills.

She was an excellent cook, if she did say so herself. Surely that would be another check in her favor. What single man wouldn't want someone who had hot meals ready for him every single night?

"I expect you to care for Iris during my working hours which I already went over with you on the phone," he went on. "I don't expect you to cook every meal, that's a duty we can share. I do need you to drive if we go out, as I'm still recovering from an accident that has limited my activities. If all of this is fine with you, then you can stay."

Darcy nodded, though she wanted to ask about his injury. But now wasn't the time and if she stayed on as nanny, she'd most likely discover what had happened to him.

"I'm fine with that deal."

She held out a hand to shake. He darted his gaze down to her hand, then back up to her face. With an emotionless expression, Colin slid his warm, strong hand into hers and an electric sensation shot straight up her arm. His eyes widened for the briefest of moments. The grip on her hand tightened.

This wasn't happening. No way could an attraction form so quickly, be so intense. She'd been convinced the tension and fascination was one-sided. Apparently not.

Darcy swallowed, wondering what he was thinking, feeling. She didn't want the awkwardness to settle between them. This was only day one, though, so she'd chalk it up to them getting a feel for each other…not the chemistry that was growing and already causing problems.

"Do you want to give me a tour of the house?" Darcy asked, needing to remove herself from temptation.

Colin blinked, dropped her hand and nodded. "Of course. I also wanted to let you know that if you need an evening off to go out or have some personal time, just give me notice. I don't expect you to put your life on hold and work twenty-four hours a day."

Laughter bubbled up and Darcy couldn't keep it contained. Colin's brows drew together.

"You find that funny?"

Waving a hand in the air, Darcy shook her head. "I have no social life. I won't require any time off."

He tipped his chin down slightly, causing a longer strand of dark hair to fall over his eye as he studied her. "You keep surprising me."

Besides his striking looks, Colin had a voice that would make any woman tremble with need. She didn't want to tremble, didn't want to have any type of unexpected attraction toward this man or any other. From here on out, until her agency was back in business, Darcy vowed to stay focused. No men, regardless of how lonely she was. She didn't need someone to complete her, not by any means. But there were those nights she missed being held, missed the powerful touch only a man could provide.

"I'm really pretty simple," she told him. "My work keeps me happy so I don't need anything else."

"What about friends? Boyfriends?"

Okay, that wasn't subtle. Was he asking as an employer or as a man?

Pulling her self-control up front and center, Darcy stepped away from him and headed out of the kitchen. "How about that tour while Iris is sleeping?"

Two weeks and a great deal of sexual tension later, Colin led Darcy down the hall toward the back of the house, well aware of her closeness behind him and even more aware of the unspoken attraction that seemed to be hovering between them. He'd been struggling to keep any emotions hidden. He didn't want her to look at him and see any sign of lust. Colin had no room for such things, not when he and his daughter were desperate for help.

But each time he'd seen Darcy with Iris, something had moved in him. Something he couldn't identify. He assumed at this point she had no boyfriend. She'd made no mention of one even though she'd never come out and answered him when he'd grilled her on the subject her first day.

She'd managed to put him in his place without a word. Fine. He didn't have time to get involved in her personal life and he sure as hell shouldn't want to.

Earlier today, when he'd mentioned working out, he'd seen a brief interest pass over her face. He figured if he showed her the gym and they both made use of it, maybe they could work through…whatever this was brewing between them. He couldn't speak for Darcy, but fourteen days of strain and sexual tension was taking its toll on him.

Colin headed toward the back of the house where the first floor bedroom had been turned into a gym. He'd specified to his designer all the equipment he'd need to continue his therapy on his own and to keep in shape. He had to keep his workouts inside now since his injuries prevented him from going out for a run or rock climbing. He'd never rock climb again. His one main passion in life had been stolen from him.

Shoving aside unwanted anger and frustration, Colin eased the French doors open and stepped inside.

"I know you're busy with Iris, but I wanted you to know this is available to you any time you want to use it. I have weights, a treadmill, elliptical, bike, all top of the line."

"Wow, you certainly take the meaning of home gym to a whole new level." Darcy glanced through the room and smiled. "I've never had much time to devote to a workout before."

Colin didn't think she needed to work out at all, but he wanted to extend the offer since he'd been using the gym and he hadn't invited her to make use of the space yet. Darcy's shapely body was perfect from every angle…and he'd studied it at every opportunity since the moment she moved in.

"You're more than welcome to everything in here if you decide you'd like to try," he told her.

"I've never used any of these machines before," she muttered. "But I'm sure I could muddle my way through."

Or he could offer to show her.

Colin cursed himself. If they were both going to use this space, he knew they had to do so at different times. The last thing he needed to see was a sweaty, flushed Darcy because that would conjure up a whole host of other images and fantasies.

At this point, he had to get something out in the open. They'd gone two weeks with passing glances and innocent touching as they worked with Iris. Each day he found it more difficult to quash his desires. And Darcy was a damn good nanny, so getting rid of her was not an option.

"I need to be honest with you," he told her.

Tucking her long hair behind her ears, Darcy nodded. "Okay."

"You're a beautiful woman," he began, hoping he wasn't making a mistake. "There's a pull between us and I don't think I'm being presumptuous when I say that. However, I plan to remain single and I have every intention of keeping our relationship professional."

Darcy's mouth had dropped open. For a moment he wondered if he'd gone too far or if his imagination had taken over.

Upfront and honest was how he preferred everything. Okay, obviously there were exceptions since he was keeping a colossal truth from her. But his royal status wouldn't affect her life. She was a nanny, she'd get paid, they would part ways in less than six months and their personal lives could remain private, for the most part.

"Then I'll be honest, too." She laced her fingers in front of her and lifted her chin. "I won't deny the attraction. I mean, you have to know what you look like, but that's just superficial. I still don't know you very well because you're so quiet and brooding, but my main focus is Iris. I promise I'm not here looking for anything other than a job. I've had enough difficulties in my life the past few years. Does that help ease your mind?"

Part of him wanted to know what she'd been through, but the other part told him to shut up and deal with his own issues. Had she just called him brooding? He suppressed the urge to smile at her bluntness. Admiration for this woman who wasn't afraid to speak her mind mixed right along with his arousal where she was concerned. The combination of the two could prove to be crippling if he didn't keep a tight rein on his emotions.

Still, Darcy wasn't like any woman he'd ever known. She wasn't blatantly sexual, she wasn't throwing herself at him even though she'd admitted to being attracted, and she'd been in his house ample time to try her hand at seduction. Not once had she come out with skimpy pajamas or purposely been provocative to try to capture his attention. Perhaps that was just another reason he found her so intriguing and refreshing.

Would she be so controlled if she knew who he really was, how much he was worth?

Being a member of royalty had always made him an instant magnet for women. His late wife hadn't cared about his status, which was one of the things that had initially drawn him to her. But then reality had hit, and the accident that nearly claimed his life wedged between them at the same time she'd discovered her pregnancy. Months of stress and worry had torn them apart and for once in his life, money couldn't fix his problems.

"You okay?" Darcy asked.

Her delicate hand rested on his bare arm and Colin clenched his teeth, fighting away the memories. He couldn't live in the past, trying to pinpoint the exact moment his marriage went wrong. Like everything else, little things started adding up to bigger things and, slowly, the marriage had just dissolved.

Iris was his main concern now. He needed to

relax, work on being a regular father giving his daughter the best life possible.

And to decide whether to renounce his title. The pressure of knowing that their wayward cousin, who didn't deserve the title, would have it if something happened to Stefan was overwhelming. He hated being in this position, but ignoring it wouldn't make the situation go away.

"Colin?"

Nodding, he let out a sigh. "I'm fine," he assured her, hating when her hand slid away. Those gentle fingertips trailed down his arm before leaving him wanting more than just an innocent touch. "Anything you want to ask about the equipment while I'm here with you?"

Her eyes roamed over the apparatus in the workout room. An image of her sweating with him flashed through his mind which led to other images of them sweating and he cursed himself. If he didn't get control over his libido he'd have more trouble on his hands than he could possibly handle.

"If I wanted to start working out, what would you recommend? The treadmill? I'm pretty out of shape."

Out of shape? Everything about her shape screamed perfection. He never was one of those guys who needed his woman to be supermodel thin. He preferred having plenty of curves to explore.

When her eyes came back to his, he fought the urge to pull her inside and get that sweat going. He'd bet his royal, jeweled crown she would look even sexier all flushed, with a sheen of perspiration across her body.

"Do you really want to work out?" he asked. "I don't want you to feel pressured. I'm just offering the room to you."

Darcy shrugged. "I could stand to lose a few pounds."

Anger simmered beneath the surface. "Who told you that?"

Darcy entered the room and checked out the elliptical, the treadmill, the free weights. "He's no longer in the picture, but that's not what matters. What matters is that I've let myself go, and with all of this at my fingertips I don't see why I shouldn't take advantage of it while I'm here."

Colin stepped in and came up behind her, close enough to touch. He clenched his hands at his sides. "If you want to feel better about yourself, that's one thing. If you're doing this because some bastard told you you're overweight, then I have a problem."

Her shoulders stiffened as she turned. The second she realized how close they were, her eyes widened, but she didn't step back. Their bodies were only a breath apart and with each inhale, the tips of her breasts brushed against his chest. He was playing with fire and damn if he could stop himself. He'd always lived for the adrenaline rush and Darcy got his blood pumping.

Being this close he noticed a sprinkling of freckles across her nose. There was so much innocence in this woman, yet in some ways she seemed too tough to be innocent. She'd gone through hard times, according to her. Even if she hadn't said so, he could tell by the way she was headstrong, determined and focused. How the hell could he not find that completely sexy?

"My weight may have been mentioned in my last relationship," she told him, keeping her eyes on his. "But he's history and I want to do this for me. Will you help me or not?"

Would he help her? Close quarters, alone without Iris as a buffer and having Darcy's body as his sole focus for hours? He may not want this attraction, but it was there nonetheless and only an idiot would turn her down.

"I'll help you," he told her. "We'll start tonight after Iris goes to bed. That work for you?"

Her smile spread across her face, lighting up those expressive eyes. "It works if you take it easy on me."

Oiktirmon. Mercy.

"Oh, I plan on giving you just what you need."

Four

What had she been thinking? Darcy had been so impressed by the gym she'd opened her mouth before she could even think about what she was saying. Now she'd committed to exercising with someone who should be posing for calendars sans shirt, while she looked like the before picture on a Weight Watcher's ad.

She'd been taken with Colin and his blunt declaration of attraction. Apparently a lust-filled haze had clouded her mind and hindered her common sense. He'd called out the obvious and now they both had to deal with the tension that would no doubt envelop them every time they were together.

Dinner had been comfortable, though. Iris as the focal point certainly helped. Now she was bathed and in bed, and Darcy had pulled on her favorite yoga pants and an old Loving Hands T-shirt. After pulling on her worn tennis shoes, she headed toward the gym.

The whirring of the treadmill filtered out of the partially open doors and into the hallway. When Darcy peeked around the corner, she was so, so glad she had the advantage of being behind him. Obvious eye-candy images aside, she was thankful no one could see her because there was no way she could take in this male form, all sweaty, shirtless and in action, and not stand here with her mouth open, eyes wide.

The full view of his tattoo caught her attention. A dragon started over one shoulder blade, swirled down one biceps and disappeared over his shoulder to the front. Her fingers itched to trace the pattern, to feel all that taut skin beneath her fingertips. Surely there was some meaning behind the image. Most people had tattoos based on something personal in their lives. She couldn't help but wonder if she'd ever uncover anything beneath the surface with him.

Just as Darcy eased the door open, Colin stumbled, shouted a curse and smacked the red emergency button on the treadmill. Gripping the sides of the machine, he panted, head hanging between his shoulders.

"Are you all right?" she asked, crossing to the piece of equipment in case he needed help.

Colin jerked his head around, wincing as he caught sight of her. "I thought you'd be longer with putting Iris down."

As he turned completely and started to step down, his leg went out from under him and he collapsed, landing hard on the belt of the machine.

Darcy squatted beside him, her hands resting on his bare knee. "Colin, are you okay?" she repeated.

Stupid question, as he'd obviously hurt himself and was trying to hide the fact. Still, she couldn't just stand here and not do or say something.

"Fine," he bit out through gritted teeth. "I'm supposed to walk every day, but the doctor says if I feel like it I can try jogging."

"Is that why you were running full speed on an incline when I came in?"

His eyes met hers. There went that click once again when this man stared at her. The intensity of his gaze couldn't even be put into words because she'd never experienced such a force in her life.

"I'm not going to be held prisoner by this injury." His tone left no room for argument. "And I don't want your pity."

Colin's eyes held hers another second before they dropped to her hands on his knee. The dark hair on his leg slid beneath her palms as she started to remove her hands. Instantly, his hand covered hers, holding her in place.

"I wasn't feeling pity," she whispered. "Attracted, intrigued, yes. Not pity."

His thumb stroked the back of her hand. "This can't be an issue."

She knew he wasn't referring to his injury or the fact that she'd found him in a state of pain.

"It's already an issue," she retorted, not even trying to pretend she had no idea what he was referring to. "We just have to take control of the tension instead of it controlling us."

His eyes held hers, the muscle ticked in his jaw. "Are you ready to get sweaty?"

Darcy swallowed, then took her own advice and tried to get a grip. Offering a smile, she said, "If you're trying to keep this attraction on the backburner, I think you probably shouldn't ask questions like that."

Laughing, Colin started to rise. "Just wanted to see the look on your face."

The man actually laughed. And there went that zing of desire shooting through her again, because a brooding Colin was sexy, but a smiling Colin was flat-out irresistible.

Darcy came to her feet. "I'm sure I didn't disappoint," she joked.

As Colin got his feet beneath him, Darcy took a step back. "So what are you recovering from?"

Raking a hand through his hair, Colin sighed and shook his head. "A life I've left behind," he muttered.

Curiosity heightened, she wanted to know more about this mysterious man who'd so easily and swiftly captured her attention.

"Tell me what your goal is," he said, resting a hand on the rail of the treadmill. "Are you wanting to lose weight, tone up or just work on feeling better about yourself?"

"All of the above."

A wide smile stretched across his face. The combination of those bright blue eyes and that knee-weakening smile could have any woman throwing all morals and professional behavior out the window.

"Let's get started," he said, clasping his hands together.

An hour later, Darcy was questioning her sanity and wondering why she'd let those sexy, dark-skinned muscles sway her judgment. How in the world did she think she could keep up? This man was obviously in shape and she was obviously… not.

She resisted the urge to bend over and pull in much-needed air to her overexerted lungs.

"Ready for more?" he asked, hands on his hips, devastatingly handsome smile on his face.

She sent him a glare. "I'm not a masochist."

"You're honest," he replied, using his T-shirt to wipe the sweat off his brow. "I prefer honesty."

"That makes two of us."

He moved over to the small refrigerator in the corner of the room and pulled out two bottles of water. After handing her one, they both uncapped the drinks and took long pulls. Water had never tasted so good.

"So why the nanny business?" he asked, propping his foot upon a workout bench. His elbow rested on his knee, the bottle of water hung between two fingers. "Because you're an amazing cook. Dinner was pretty damn delicious. All of the meals have been great, but tonight's was my favorite."

Stunned and flattered at the compliment and his openness, Darcy screwed the lid back on her bottle. "I've never known anything other than taking care of children. I went to work with my grandmother every single day and fell in love. Cooking is a fun hobby and I love trying out new things. I guess if I weren't a nanny, I'd like to be a chef or a caterer."

She'd quickly steered the conversation to cooking. Anything to avoid talking too much about babies. The facts that children of her own weren't in her future and that anything she'd saved toward adoption had disappeared with Thad cut deep. Still, taking care of others was what she was meant to be doing, of that she was sure.

"Hey." Colin tipped his head to the side, searching her face. "You all right?"

"Oh, yeah." Darcy pushed a sweaty strand of hair that had escaped her ponytail behind her ear. "Just tired."

Pushing off the bench, Colin stalked closer, his focus solely on her. "Tomorrow we'll do weights and skip cardio."

"Tomorrow?" she asked. "You mean we're going to do this every day?"

The corner of his mouth twitched. "Only if you want to. I'm here every night after Iris goes to bed. If you want to join me, you are more than welcome. If you don't want to, no pressure. Personally, I think you're perfect the way you are."

"You haven't seen me naked," she muttered, realizing her mistake the second the words were out of her mouth. "Sorry. I'm—forget I said that."

"When a woman as sultry as you says the word *naked* it's impossible to keep certain images from flooding my mind."

Darcy held onto her bottle, thankful for the prop because her hands were shaking, as were her knees, and her entire body was responding to that low, sexy, heavily accented voice.

"Where are you from?" she asked.

"Greece."

Of course he was. Someplace beautiful and exotic, much like the man himself.

"So, dinner requests for tomorrow?" she asked. "I'll probably need to run to the store at some point, if that's okay."

"Not a problem." He turned toward the doorway, motioning her to exit ahead of him. "I have no requests. You obviously know what you're doing in the kitchen, which is more than I can say for myself."

Stepping into the hallway, she waited until Colin reached in and turned off the light. Darkness enveloped them, save for the slash of light at the end of the hallway shining down from the chandelier in the foyer.

"What's your favorite food?" she asked, trying to focus on his face in the dark, though neither of them had made a move to walk into the light.

"I haven't had too many American dishes," he replied. "I normally eat a lot of fish and vegetables."

Which would further explain why he was so

buff and polished, and she had more dimples than a newborn baby's backside.

"I know just what to serve," she replied.

Her vision had adjusted to the darkness enough to see the flare of heat in his baby blues just as he stepped in closer. "You claim I can't deliver loaded statements." His rich, low voice washed over her already heated body, ironically sending shivers all through her. "I'd say that goes both ways."

Before she could respond, Colin trailed a fingertip along the side of her face.

"Wh—what are you doing?" she asked, cursing her stammer, knowing it was a sign of weakness.

"Putting my curiosity to rest."

"Curiosity?"

That finger kept stroking, causing every pleasure point in her body to tingle.

"I needed to know if you are as silky as you appear," he murmured.

Warmth radiated from his broad body as he leaned in even closer, close enough to brush against hers and have her backing up into the wall.

Her gaze held his. "Am I?"

"Here you are," he whispered. "I wonder about here."

His lips covered hers in an instant, leaving her no choice but to reply to his demands. Okay, she could've chosen to push him away, but…why?

His tongue swept inside her mouth just as his hand curved around her chin, his thumb and forefinger on either side of her face as if to hold her in place. Darcy arched into him, wanting more and taking all he delivered. So many promises wrapped in that one kiss and all she had to do was let go.

Hadn't they both agreed to keep this professional? There was nothing professional about the spiral of arousal coursing through her or the need she so desperately wanted to cave in to.

Colin lifted only to shift his stance, pressing her further against the wall and his very hard, impressive body. Whoever Colin Alexander was, the man possessed power and control. He demanded so much without words and his actions proved he was used to getting what he wanted.

Just like Thad.

Darcy jerked her head to the side, causing Colin's lips to slide against her jaw, his hand falling away.

She closed her eyes, trying to ignore the devil on her shoulder telling her to turn back and let Colin continue whatever it was he had in mind.

"Colin…"

He dropped his forehead to her shoulder, sighed, then took a step back. "Darcy, that was inexcusable."

Holding her hand to her moist lips, Darcy risked glancing back to Colin. "No, no. We're both to blame."

He propped his hands on his narrow hips and stared up at the ceiling. Darcy had no idea what to say, what to do.

"I've never been in this position before," she told him, clutching her water and wrapping her arms around her waist. "You need to know that I don't kiss employers and I've never, ever had a relationship with any of them beyond a professional one."

"I believe you."

When he offered no further comment, Darcy couldn't take the uncomfortable silence any longer. She turned and started walking down the hallway, when he called her name. She froze, but didn't look back.

"You need to know the last person I had a relationship with was my wife." His soft words floated down the wide hall, enveloping her. "I know we aren't taking this any further, but I didn't want you to think I made a habit of coming on to beautiful women."

Beautiful women.

Darcy threw him a look over her shoulder, nodded and carried on. She didn't stop, didn't slow down until she was in her room with the door shut behind her. Her heart still pounded just as fiercely as it had when she'd been in the darkened hall with Colin, the same as when she'd been sweating in the gym with him and the same as when he'd opened the door first thing that morning looking all rumpled and sexy.

With baby monitors in every room, there was no way she'd miss it if Iris needed something. Which was a very good thing because when Colin had been kissing her, for the briefest of moments, she'd forgotten her sole purpose for even being here. Her mind had traveled to a selfish place and all she wanted was more of that talented, demanding mouth on hers.

Dropping her head back against the door, Darcy groaned. This was the last thing she needed. If she didn't straighten up and focus, she'd have to resign and she needed the full amount of money Colin was paying her if she wanted to keep the agency afloat in any way. Not to mention if she wanted to ever get an apartment or a reliable vehicle.

The video monitor on the white nightstand showed a very peaceful Iris hugging her new doll to her chest. It was in the quiet, serene moments like this that Darcy truly felt that void in her heart. Growing up around other children and loving families, Darcy had always assumed she'd have a family of her own one day.

With the way she worked herself now, though, she didn't even have time for a date, much less a husband. Losing her entire savings had only pushed her dream of adopting further back, making her wonder if she just wasn't meant to be a mother.

There were worse things in the world than not having children...though from her perspective not many. She truly wished with all her heart that she had the ability to conceive like nearly every other woman, but that wasn't meant to be and she had to quit dwelling on it and move on. She wanted to be happy, so she had to focus on happy things and things that were in her control...infertility was certainly not one of them.

Tomorrow, she vowed, she would be one hundred percent professional. She just had to figure out a way to become immune to those striking blue eyes, that sultry accent and forget the way his lips basically assaulted hers in the best, most arousing way possible.

Hysterical laughter escaped her. Sure. No problem.

Five

The alarm chimed throughout the house, indicating that someone had triggered the gate and was coming up the drive. Colin lifted Iris in his arms and headed to the door to help Darcy with her grocery bags. She'd been gone for quite a while and he wondered if she'd run away or if she was stockpiling for the next month.

He'd just gotten off the phone with his assistant who informed Colin of some rather interesting information regarding Darcy and her financial situation. Apparently she was much worse off than he'd first thought. He wasn't sure whether to bring it up or let it slide. The last thing he wanted to do was make her uncomfortable or embarrassed, but at the same time, he wanted to do…something.

He was definitely going to have to bring up the fact her business was basically failing, but he needed to figure out the delicate matter.

Colin didn't know her personal issues, and he had no doubt she had them with her financial situation. All he knew right now was that her business had hit hard times in the last year and had fallen from one of the most sought out to an agency with only Darcy as the worker. There was definitely a story there.

When he opened the door, he didn't see her car. Instead, Darcy was walking up the drive, her arms weighted down with reusable grocery sacks bulging with food.

He sat Iris on the stoop. "Stay here, baby. Daddy needs to help Darcy."

With the gated property, Colin wasn't concerned about Iris wandering off. Worst-case scenario, she'd pluck all the vibrant flowers in the beds before he could get back to her. There was a pool around back, but he'd watch her and make sure she didn't toddle around the house.

Quickly moving toward Darcy, Colin felt his

blood pressure rising. "What the hell are you doing?" he asked once he'd closed the gap. "Where's your car?"

"Broke down about a half mile back."

He pulled several bags off each arm, narrowing his eyes at the red creases on her delicate skin caused by all the weight. She wasn't some damn pack mule.

"Why didn't you call me?" he demanded as he curled his hands around the straining handles. "I would've come to get you."

Left with only two lighter bags, Darcy smiled and started up the drive. "By the time you could've gotten Iris in the car seat and gotten to me, I would've been here. Plus I didn't want to bother you guys in case you were playing or she was getting fussy and ready to lie down for a nap."

Even though Darcy's hair was pulled up into a high ponytail, Colin noted the damp tendrils clinging to her neck. The heat of the California sun could be relentless.

"Where exactly is your car?" he asked, trying to keep his voice controlled.

She explained what street she'd left it on, which

really didn't mean much to him since he knew little about the area or the street names. He'd call to have it towed and then he'd work on getting her proper transportation. No way was any employee of his going to be stranded again.

What if Iris had been with Darcy? Then what would she have done? The mishap was frustrating on so many levels.

Not only was she his employee, he refused to see any woman working herself to the point of sweaty exhaustion and that's exactly where Darcy was at. A sheen of perspiration glistened across her forehead and upper lip, her cheeks were red and she had circles beneath her eyes.

Where he was from the women would never leave their homes without full makeup, perfectly styled hair and flashy clothes...much like LA. Still, Darcy didn't seem to care that she wasn't completely made up for an outing. He actually found the quality quite refreshing and incredibly hot.

As if he needed another reason to be aroused by her. He needed to nip this sexual urge in the bud and stay focused.

Once they reached the stoop, Iris had indeed

plucked up a variety of flowers, clutching them in her tight little hand.

"Pitty," she exclaimed, thrusting them toward Darcy. "You pitty."

Darcy laughed. "Oh, honey. You're so sweet."

Colin looked at Darcy and saw an alluring, determined and resilient woman. How could any man not be attracted to those qualities? And her sexuality was stealthy. You didn't see the impact coming until it hit you hard. Each day that passed made him realize just how much power she was beginning to have over him.

By the time they got all the bags inside and onto the wide center island in the kitchen, Colin had worked up quite a sweat of his own.

"I'll put these away," Darcy told him as she opened the pantry. "I need to walk back to my car after and see if it's the transmission. I've been having issues with that thing, but a transmission would cost more than the old car is worth."

Colin stood amazed. "*You* plan on looking to see if the transmission is shot?"

Over the stacks of bags, Darcy met his gaze. "Yeah, why? Who else is going to look at it?"

Iris patted his leg and Colin leaned down to

lift her up. She still clutched those colorful flowers in her hand so he moved to the cabinet to get down a small glass to use as a vase.

"I'd call a mechanic," he replied, filling the glass with water.

With a soft laugh and shake of her head, Darcy turned her attention back to pulling the groceries from the sacks. "Well, mechanics charge just to come look at the car, then there's the labor to fix the problem, plus the part."

As she listed all the costs associated with getting the vehicle fixed, Colin had to remind himself he wasn't back at the palace. He wasn't talking to someone who would just pay someone else to take care of the issue and move on. Darcy was obviously a hard worker and she didn't need to tell him her funds were lacking.

Taking the flowers from Iris's hand, he sat them in the glass. "There, sweetheart."

She clapped her hands together and wiggled in an attempt to get away. Carefully, he put her back down and watched her move to Darcy. The easy way Iris had taken to the new nanny made him happy he'd allowed her to stay. The incident in the hall last night, though, had kept him up questioning his decision. They were still on a trial and he really didn't want to start the process of finding someone else. That was one thing he wouldn't do to Iris. Even though they'd moved across the globe, he wanted Iris to have as much stability in her life as possible until he was absolutely certain of their future.

"Hey, cutie." Darcy pulled out a bag of flour and glanced down to her side, a wide smile stretching across her face. "I'm almost done and then you and I can play a little game."

"I'll take care of getting your car picked up."

Darcy's eyes flashed back to his. "That's not your job."

Crossing his arms over his chest, ready for the battle she so obviously thought was coming, Colin replied, "Cooking every single meal and going to the store isn't your job, either. I'm trying to help. We agreed on sharing these responsibilities."

"You can help by letting me do what works for me with my personal circumstances. Fixing my car wasn't included in our agreement."

As Darcy ignored him to focus on putting the last of the groceries away, Colin didn't know if he was pissed to be dismissed so easily or if he was elated that she wasn't walking on egg-shells around him because he was a prince. How would she react if she knew just how wealthy he was? Would she even care about his royal status? Darcy didn't seem the type to be attracted to money or power. She seemed to be doing just fine on her own.

And that was the main problem he was having. She shouldn't have to do everything on her own.

"How about I fix lunch and you can make dinner?" he suggested.

Bundling all the reusable sacks into one neatly folded pile, Darcy raised a brow and grinned. "And what are you making for lunch, oh great chef?"

"You're mocking me," he laughed. "I know I'm not as good as you in the kitchen, but I think I can give you a run for your money. Isn't that the expression you Americans have?"

Her lips pursed as she continued to stare. "It is, but I don't think you can hold your own against me."

"Challenge accepted," he told her, ready to prove her wrong.

Damn it. Now he needed to search on the internet for something easy, quick and delicious. He'd been thinking of throwing sandwich stuff together for lunch, but given her instant doubt, Colin had to raise his game. And he would, just as soon as he took care of the car. She was getting his assistance whether she liked it or not.

The shrill alarm had Darcy jumping to her feet and pulling Iris with her. They'd been coloring on the floor in the living room when the ear-piercing noise came out of nowhere.

Darcy knew that sound and it was all she could do not to laugh. Calmly, though, she rested Iris on her hip and headed toward the kitchen where lunch was probably not going to be happening anytime soon.

Standing in the wide, arched doorway, Darcy took in the scene and had to literally bite her lips to keep from laughing.

There were dirty bowls littering the island, opened packages of random ingredients spread about and Colin was currently slapping a kitchen towel at the small flame coming from the burner. Smoke billowed through the open space as Darcy moved into the kitchen. She eased Iris into her high chair and wheeled it over near the patio door, which Darcy opened to let some fresh air in. She made her way down the wall, opening each window as she passed.

Colin turned, still holding the charred dish-towel, and shrugged. "I'm not admitting defeat."

"Of course not," she replied, not even bothering to hide her smile. "Why would you?"

"Lunch will be just a few more minutes."

"I'm sure it will be wonderful." Darcy shrugged. "No rush."

Poor guy was still trying to save his pride. She wasn't about to say more. Their easy banter seriously helped take the edge off the sexual tension. Playfulness, even a little flirting she could handle. Anything beyond that…she glanced to the tiny flame Colin was smacking. Yeah, that flame signified her life right now. If she got too close to Colin she'd get burned. The signs were literally in front of her face.

Darcy had just grabbed a handful of puffed snacks to hold Iris over until lunch was ready when another alarm sounded through the house. This one was announcing a visitor.

The darn house was wired so tight with security and monitors and alarms, Darcy's head had practically spun in circles when Colin had explained the entire system to her. Who was this man that he needed so much security?

"Are you expecting company?" she asked, laying the snacks across the highchair tray for Iris.

"Actually, I am." Colin turned off the burner, sat the pan on a cooler one and turned to her. "Don't touch anything. I've got it under control. This won't take long."

He rushed from the room and out the front door.

"Your father is one mysterious man," Darcy muttered to Iris. "And apparently not a chef."

Smoothing the dark curls away from the baby's face, Darcy really studied how much Iris looked like Colin. All bronzed skin, dark molasses eyes and striking features. Iris would be an absolute bombshell when she grew up. Darcy couldn't help but wonder if Iris's mother had been a Greek beauty as well. Most likely Colin wouldn't have married someone who was an ogre.

Moments later, Colin breezed back into the

house. "Sorry about that. Lunch will be ready in five minutes if you'd like to get some plates out."

"Are you going to tell me what we're having now?"

"You'll see," he told her before he went back into the foyer.

On a sigh, she crossed the room and pulled out two plates and one smaller plate for Iris. She resisted the urge to stroke the beautiful cabinets and the quartz countertops. This kitchen alone cost more money than she made in a year...during the good times. Having a home and a gourmet kitchen with a family to cook for was a dream she honestly didn't see coming true. That was okay, though. For now she was here, working and making money to save her agency, and in the end that's all that truly mattered. And the fact she was caring for a baby was a great form of forced therapy she'd desperately needed to face her fears.

Moments later, Colin came back into the kitchen wearing a mischievous grin, but he said nothing as he dished out whatever he'd managed to salvage from the burning pan. Apparently he'd removed the pot before the flames consumed their entire meal.

"I admit, after the fanfare with the smoke alarm, this actually smells delicious."

He threw her a glance over his shoulder. "I have a whole host of surprises for you."

Those words held a plethora of meanings, but when said while holding her gaze beneath heavy lids, her mind instantly traveled to the darkened hallway last night and how her body still ached after such a gloriously arousing kiss.

Could such an experience be labeled by one simple word? A kiss was something that could be given from a parent to a child, from a child to a pet, from a peasant to the hand of a diplomat. The word *kiss* blanketed a lot of ground.

"Ready?"

Darcy blinked, realizing Colin stood in front of her with two plates of…

"You made shrimp Alfredo?" she asked, more than amazed.

"You think I can't boil noodles and melt some butter?" he asked, feigning shock.

Taking her plate, inhaling the garlicky goodness, she laughed. "I had my doubts."

Darcy sat her plate on the table and went to move Iris's highchair over.

"I've got her," Colin said, holding his hand up. "You eat while it's hot."

Darcy stared as Colin wheeled Iris closer to the table. She then sat in amazement as he cut up the noodles, blew on them and offered small bites to his daughter.

"You're not eating," he commented without turning his head in her direction.

"I'm surprised." Darcy slid onto the built-in bench beneath the wide window. Grabbing her fork, she started pushing the noodles and shrimp around on her plate. "I'm the nanny, so eating a hot meal isn't something I'm used to. I'm also not used to the parent doing my job while I'm sitting right here."

He tossed her a glance. "I'm not like most parents. She's my daughter and I'm not paying you to raise her so I can prop my feet up and watch her life go by. I'm paying you to help for a few months. There's a huge difference."

Darcy swallowed, hating how her observation instantly made him defensive and how she was reminded again how little time she would actually have here.

"I apologize," she said, stabbing a plump shrimp coated in Alfredo sauce. "I should know by now that every family, every circumstance is different."

"Don't apologize," he replied. "Actually, as soon as you're finished eating, I have something for you."

Intrigued, Darcy stared across the table. "You made lunch, you're forcing me to eat instead of feeding Iris and you have something else up your sleeve? You've got to be kidding."

The muscle in his jaw ticked, his eyes held hers. "I don't joke too often."

The man was intense, she'd give him that. He went from super dad to sexy employer in the span of one quick blink. Regardless of his demeanor, Colin Alexander exuded sex appeal.

Darcy didn't ask any more questions. She didn't know Colin well, but she was positive anything she'd ask would be dodged or ignored. He was a man of absolute control, absolute power. She had no clue what he did for a living, she only knew he worked from home. However Colin made his money, Darcy was positive he dominated every facet of his life, and was even more controlled and possibly ruthless in whatever business he was in.

They finished lunch in silence, except for the cute noises and random words coming from Iris. When Darcy was finished, she took the plates to the sink, rinsed them and put them in the dishwasher.

"This is a really nice dishwasher."

Inwardly she groaned. What sane person coveted someone else's kitchen appliances? Talk about pathetic. She was showing her lower-class side…which was the only side she knew lately.

Pulling the tray out, Colin lifted Iris and carefully set her on the tile. In an instant she darted off toward the living room. Thanks to the mostly open-concept design of the house, they could still keep an eye on her through the wide, arched doorway.

The little girl picked up the doll Darcy had given her, sat on the floor and started rocking her. That familiar ache spread through Darcy. But there were plenty more blessings in her life to count. Each day with Iris was a blessing. The child was sweet, always happy and fun-loving, when she got her naps in, and Darcy was lucky to be working under such amazing circumstances.

"Get Iris and meet me out front."

Darcy glanced back to Colin. "You're making me nervous."

One corner of his mouth kicked up. "Baby, that's the best compliment anyone has ever given me."

He strode away without another word and Darcy had a gut feeling she'd just stirred the hornet's nest of hormones.

Darcy crossed into the living room and slid her hands beneath Iris's little arms. "Come on, sweetheart. Bring your dolly and let's go see what your daddy is up to."

"Doll," Iris repeated. "Pitty."

Laughing, Darcy kissed the dark head of curls. "Yes, baby. Your dolly is pretty."

Stepping outside, Darcy immediately spotted Colin with a wide grin on his face.

"What is that?" she asked, glancing over his shoulder at the big, black SUV, all shiny and brand-new.

"Yours."

Six

Colin watched Darcy as her eyes widened, her face paled.

"You—what…"

Her stuttering and the fact she was rendered speechless had him confused. "Your car isn't worth fixing and you need viable transportation. Consider this a very late birthday present."

Her eyes darted to his and instead of gratitude he saw…anger? Seriously? He didn't know a woman that didn't fawn all over gifts, especially a new car. He didn't know where he'd gone wrong here, but he'd seriously miscalculated her response.

"You said you'd call someone about my car," she explained.

"I did. I had it removed from the road and now you have a new vehicle that you won't have to worry about."

Darcy didn't look nearly as excited as he'd figured she would. In fact, she looked downright angry.

"I can't accept this," she stated, still remaining on the concrete stoop holding onto Iris. "I want my own car fixed, not a replacement that cost more than I could ever afford. And I don't need a birthday present from you."

"If you don't want it as a late present, then just use the vehicle while you work for me," he said slowly, moving toward her as he made sure she understood this wasn't any form of bribery or something more. "Consider it one of the incentives I mentioned on your first day. The vehicle is not up for debate. You need to have reliable transportation because you're watching my daughter and had she been in your car earlier, you both would've been stranded."

Darcy rolled her eyes. "Don't be so dramatic. I wasn't stranded. I walked here. Had Iris been with me, I would've called for help and you could've been there in no time. I was only a half mile away."

"What happens when you're ten miles away?" he countered, slipping Iris from Darcy's arms. "You can't walk that far with a toddler and you can't stay in the car in this heat."

Darcy crossed her arms over her chest and glanced away. "I can handle myself."

"Do you even want to go look at the car?" he asked.

"I can see it just fine." She brought her eyes back up to meet his. "I would like to know where my car is and I want it back."

Spinning on her heel, she went back inside, slamming the door. Colin glanced to Iris who was now chewing on the small stuffed doll's hair.

"Where did I go wrong?" he asked.

Colin knew whatever had just happened had little to do with the vehicle in his drive and everything to do with something that was personal to her. Did her old broken car hold some sentimental value?

* * *

"We better go see if she's sticking around," he told Iris as he headed toward the door.

By the time he found Darcy, she was in her room, standing at the floor-to-ceiling window looking out onto the backyard. Her room was neat and tidy. She'd plumped the pillows on her perfectly made bed and her single piece of luggage sat on the floor at the foot of it. Other than a small pair of flip-flops, there was no sign she'd even made herself at home. He knew she was orderly around the house, but he assumed in her own room, she'd be a little more laid back.

"Are you quitting?" he asked from the doorway. Even though this was his house, the bedroom was Darcy's for as long as she was here and he wasn't about to infringe on her territory.

Without turning around, Darcy let out a laugh that held no humor. "I have nowhere else to go and I need this job. I'll use the car while I'm here, but I really just want mine back. I have my reasons."

"Down," Iris said, squirming against him.

"Can we come in?" he asked.

Darcy glanced over her shoulder. "It's your house, Colin."

He stepped into the room and closed the door, confining Iris to an area where he could still watch her and talk to Darcy at the same time.

"Listen, I had no idea getting you a car would set off so much emotion." Slowly closing the space between them, he came to stand in front of her. "I'll get your car fixed and have it delivered back here. But you will still be using the new one. No arguments."

She eyed him for another minute before tipping her head to the side. "One of these days someone is going to tell you no."

"No, no, no, no," Iris chanted as she toddled around the room waving her doll in the air.

Darcy laughed and Colin couldn't stop himself from smiling. "She's the only one who can get away with it," he informed Darcy.

Truly focusing on Darcy, he crossed the room. As he neared, her eyes widened. He liked to think it was from the attraction, but that was his arrogance talking. More than likely she was trying to figure him out, same as he was doing with her.

But he would get through her defenses. He knew without a doubt her secret had everything to do with the fact that she had nowhere else to go.

As the space between them minimized, Colin kept his gaze locked on hers. The closer he got, the more she had to tip her head back to hold his stare.

"I can't help but feel you're hiding something," he started. "Your background check told me your business has hit a rough patch and you are on your own now."

Darcy nodded, her lips thinning. "There are challenges I'm facing privately, but nothing that will affect my job with you. I promise. I just don't want to be indebted to you for fixing my car."

Money wasn't the root of all evil as the old saying went. The evil was the person holding the purse strings who did nothing to help others.

"I think I'll take Iris outside for a walk." Darcy skirted around him, careful to shift her body so she didn't even brush against him. "Feel free to join us if you want."

Colin laughed as he turned to face her. "Not very subtle, the way you dodged my question."

"Subtlety wasn't what I was going for." She lifted Iris in her arms and smiled. The way she headed straight out the door as if she hadn't just put him in his place really annoyed and amused him at the same time. Damn, she was fun, yet prickly.

Darcy was perfect with Iris, independent and she turned him inside out at every move.

When his marriage had started failing, Colin blamed himself. He'd put Karina through hell with his injury, his surgeries, not being there for her as a husband should be. He'd never imagined he'd feel a desire for another woman again, but here he was, pining after his temporary nanny, of all people.

If he didn't keep his head on straight, he'd be losing focus on why he was in LA to begin with. He was no closer to deciding if staying away from Galini Isle was best for him and Iris or if returning to the secure, enclosed, yet exposed, lifestyle of the royals was the way he should go.

Here he had more freedom to take her out in public. They'd walked to the park last week and it had been so refreshing not to have guards hovering nearby. The longer he stayed in the

United States, the more he worried he'd never want to leave.

There was only one right decision…he only wished he knew which one it was.

Playing outside in the yard was always so much fun for Darcy. She loved hearing Iris's squeals of delight and seeing her little carefree spirit. Darcy had been here for a full month now and had easily passed the trial period. Each second she spent with Iris only had Darcy more thankful she'd fought for this position. Holding onto Iris's tiny little hand just felt right. Everything about being with this sweet child felt right.

Not to mention that working for a man who oozed sexiness, power and control was one giant glob of icing on the proverbial cake.

Talk about landing the job of a lifetime. Still, Darcy couldn't help but wonder what happened to Colin's late wife. He didn't mention her, didn't even have any photos around the house. The man seemed as if he was running away or hiding from something, but she truly had no clue what. She could easily research him online, but she wasn't going to snoop into his life. That would be sneaky and Darcy prided herself on honesty. If he wanted to discuss his life, he would when the time was right.

Iris pulled away from Darcy and started running toward the landscaping framing the patio. Shielding her eyes with her hand, Darcy stared ahead as the little girl ran after a butterfly that had landed on one of the vibrant flowers. By the time Iris got there, the butterfly had flown away.

Iris looked around and when she realized the insect was no longer nearby, her chin started quivering. Closing the space between them, Darcy knelt down in front of the toddler and smoothed the curls away from her forehead, making a mental note to pick up some hair accessories for Iris.

"It's okay, sweetheart," Darcy consoled. "Miss Butterfly had to go home for a nap. I bet she'll be back another time. Would you like to go in and lie down? I saw a butterfly book in your room. How about we read that?"

"No," Iris cried, shaking her head. "No, no, no."

The one word kids learned early and used for nearly every reply, especially when they were in need of a nap. Darcy may have been working with older children these past several years, but certain things she would never forget.

When Darcy scooped her up and headed toward the house, the tears instantly transformed from sad to angry, and Iris's arms started flying as the instant tantrum went into full swing. Maybe Darcy shouldn't have taken Iris on that walk. Apparently the window of opportunity was missed and the nap should've come first.

Patting her back and trying to dodge the whirlwind arms, Darcy took Iris into the house. Of course, inside, the cries seemed to echo into surround sound. Colin came running from the office off the kitchen, his cell to his ear, worry etched across his face.

"What happened?" he said, holding the device away from his mouth.

"She's just tired," Darcy explained. "Sorry we disturbed you."

Colin didn't resume his call as Darcy walked by. Maybe he was waiting for them to pass because of Iris's ear-splitting screams, but the way he studied them, Darcy worried he was wondering why his daughter was so unhappy. This was the first time Iris had truly thrown a fit around

Darcy, but every kid had their moments and as a nanny, one just had to learn how to adjust to that child's needs accordingly.

And right now, little Miss Iris needed her bed and a couple of hours of peace and quiet.

As she reached the top of the stairs, Darcy didn't have to glance over her shoulder to know that Colin was staring at her.

"Come on, little one," Darcy cooed.

After walking around the room, shutting the blinds, turning on the small fan for white noise and grabbing Iris's blanket and doll, Darcy settled into the cushy rocking chair and began to hum, occasionally adding in a few lyrics to "You Are My Sunshine." Iris's eyes started to grow heavy. Darcy knew the rule of thumb was to lay young children down while they were still awake, but holding and rocking a baby was a temptation she couldn't avoid. Today Darcy justified it by telling herself she was just waiting for Iris to calm down.

Darcy held onto the precious bundle in her arms and came to her feet. Iris still clutched the silky blanket and stuffed doll as Darcy eased the sleeping beauty into her bed.

With her hands resting on the rail, Darcy stared at the spiky, damp lashes resting on Iris's reddened cheeks. Moments ago this child was throwing a fit and now she slept peacefully. When she woke she wouldn't remember she'd been upset, and that was how Darcy wanted to live her life.

Moving forward was the only way to prove there was life after the death of a dream. She couldn't allow endometriosis to define her. Discovering that the family she'd dreamed of having one day wouldn't happen had been a crushing blow, but Darcy had persevered, forcing herself to become stronger than her disappointments.

Swallowing the lump in her throat, Darcy turned from the bed and headed into the hall. She'd just pulled the door closed when she turned and ran straight into Colin's hard chest.

The instant force of colliding with him threw her off balance. Colin's hands immediately gripped her bare arms to steady her. Breath caught in her throat, her heart beat a fast, bruising rhythm against her chest. An instant flash of their heated kiss flooded her mind and all Darcy could think of was how perfectly they fit together.

Down girl.

Colin's eyes studied her face, her mouth. Tingles shot through her...tingles she shouldn't be feeling for her boss.

"We need to talk."

The statement, laced with such authority, delivered a punch to her stomach. Were they going to talk professionally? Personally? Was he upset with her for something she'd done?

Or did he want her alone for purely selfish, carnal reasons?

The second he turned and walked away, Darcy followed.

Seven

Fisting his hands at his sides, Colin cursed himself as he went downstairs and into his office. He had to keep reminding himself that the woman he'd hired to care for Iris was an employee, not an object to be lusting after. He'd never been sexually attracted to an employee—before, during or after his marriage.

Not once had his professional and personal needs ever crossed paths, but every single time he looked at Darcy he felt that kick to the gut that demanded he take notice of the all-American beauty.

Added to that, she was the only woman since Karina to have any connection to Iris. Colin would be lying to himself if he didn't admit that seeing Darcy around his daughter in all her youthful, vibrant glory had something tugging on his heart.

Damn it, he didn't want his heart tugged. He had too much on his plate right now and craving a woman, his nanny, for pity's sake, was not an option.

"You wanted me?"

Grinding his teeth to keep from saying what he really wanted, Colin turned to face Darcy. He'd assumed coming to his office would make this conversation easier, less personal.

"I want you to stop rocking Iris before you lay her down to sleep."

Darcy blanched and Colin cursed himself for the rough tone he'd taken.

"She was always used to just being laid down," he went on, trying to lighten his voice. It wasn't Darcy's fault he was fighting a losing battle with his attraction for her.

Darcy straightened her shoulders, tipped her chin and gave a quick nod. "I apologize. I'll be sure to lay her down right away next time."

Stiffly, she turned toward the door and Colin

hated himself for making her feel bad about herself. Damn it. He didn't want this. He didn't want the chemistry or the awkward sexual tension, and he sure as hell didn't want to have to mask his arousal by being snippy and gruff with her. He wanted Iris to have that loving touch, to be wrapped in the arms of someone who cared for her, and it was obvious Darcy cared for his little girl.

Maybe he wasn't capable of being happy anywhere if this was any indication. He'd taken out his frustrations with himself on Darcy. If he wasn't happy here, though, did that mean he wasn't happy stepping away from his duty? Is that what all of this boiled down to?

Colin had been in a great mood moments ago as he'd been talking on the phone with his best friend, Prince Luc Silva. He hadn't spoken to him in months, other than texts or emails. As soon as they'd hung up, Darcy's soft voice had filtered through the monitor system in the home and damn if hearing all of that softness wasn't like being wrapped in her sweet embrace.

He couldn't afford to be wrapped up in anything that didn't involve his country, his loyalty and the decision he needed to make regarding his and Iris's future in the kingdom.

"Darcy," he called out before she could clear the doorway.

She froze, but didn't turn around. "Yes?"

Anything he wanted to say would be a bad idea, rocking their already shaky relationship. "Nothing," he said, shaking his head.

Regardless of the attraction, Colin was glad he'd decided to let Darcy stay on after they'd verbally battled that first day. He couldn't imagine anyone else with Iris.

Each day brought them closer to the six-month mark, closer to his staying or going. And, to be honest, he was growing too fond of having her here, in his life. He was finding an inner peace he hadn't expected. He was almost angry at himself for allowing his emotions to get the better of him, but where Darcy was concerned, he was finding he had little say in the matter.

Stefan was putting the pressure on, but Colin couldn't deal with Galini Isle and Darcy simultaneously. Both issues were overwhelming and threatened to take over his life. Right now, though, he wanted to concentrate on Darcy. Even though he knew Galini Isle should come first, he needed to see if there was more to their attraction than pure lust.

After dinner, Colin wanted to give Iris her bath so Darcy took the opportunity to sew a button back on her only dress shirt. The button right at the breast had popped off after a big inhale. In order for this top to fit properly, she either needed to lose a few pounds or stop breathing. She was thankful Colin had been nowhere around to witness the mishap.

Threading the needle, Darcy quickly fixed the shirt and was putting her small sewing kit away when a knock sounded at her door.

"Come in," she called as she wound the unused thread back around the spool.

Colin stepped in, holding Iris who was wrapped in her thick terrycloth monogrammed towel. Darcy didn't even want to know how much that plush towel cost…she'd seen the designer label.

"I need to make a phone call," Colin told her, taking in the shirt in her lap and the supplies spread over the bed. "Am I interrupting something?"

"Oh, no." Darcy scooted everything out of the way and came to her feet, smoothing down her pink T-shirt. "I was just sewing a button back on my shirt."

Colin's brows drew together. "Just buy a new shirt."

Yeah, why didn't she think of that? Between being technically homeless, nearly ready to shut the doors on the business barely keeping food in her mouth and trying to keep her car running, why hadn't she just hit the mall in her spare time for a new wardrobe?

But he didn't need her sarcasm. A man like Colin wouldn't understand because if anything in his life was broken, he could just pay to have it fixed or snap his fingers and have people at his beck and call.

Another layer of division between them, showing her just how vast their differences were.

Ignoring his question, because anything she would reply with would most definitely be snarky, she came to her feet, crossed the room and reached for Iris.

"Go on and make your call." The sweet scent of

freshly bathed baby always made her heart weep just a little. "I'll take care of this sweet princess."

"Don't call her that."

Jerking her attention from the wrapped, squirming bundle in her arms to Colin, Darcy jerked. "Call her what? Princess?"

"I don't like that term," he stated, crossing his arms and leveling her gaze.

"It's a simple term of endearment," Darcy defended herself, shifting Iris to settle her more comfortably on her hip. "I'm not sure what you think I'm implying when I say it, but—"

"No more. I don't want her to be a spoiled child and that term suggests too much."

"Colin—"

He held up a hand, cutting her off once more. "She's my daughter. She will not be called princess."

Feeling her blood pressure rise through the onslaught of confusion, Darcy took a step forward. "Yes, sir. If you'll excuse me, I need to get Iris ready for bed."

She pushed by him and exited her room, headed into the nursery next door and closed the door. What on earth had gotten into him? He was still in a mood and Darcy had no clue why. Darcy quickly dressed Iris in a pair of yellow footed pajamas with little bunnies on each of the toes. Every single baby item the toddler possessed was adorable. Darcy was getting more and more used to being surrounded by everything baby. The only thing she worried about now was how she'd leave at the end of the term they'd agreed upon. Staying away from babies for years had helped to soothe her ache somewhat, but being thrust into the world of all things tiny and pink brought Darcy's wishes back to the surface. To think all of that would be taken from her again in a few months.

She had no clue what he'd do when her term was up. Perhaps he just wanted to get his feet back on solid ground since he was a widower with a baby. Maybe he thought he could take it from there. Darcy had learned long ago not to question her clients' intentions.

She couldn't get too used to the weight of Iris in her arms, or the way Iris would clutch that ugly old doll Darcy had given her or the way she had started to reach for Darcy. But such simple things had already infiltrated Darcy's heart.

And Colin, as grouchy and moody as he'd been, had also managed to capture her attention in a way she hadn't expected. She couldn't get the image of him dominating her, kissing her, demanding more, from her mind.

As Darcy turned off the lights and clicked on the projector that danced stars across the ceiling, she knew she needed to find him and figure out what was going on. The man was a walking mystery, and if she was going to stay, and she really had no choice, she needed to clear the air. He obviously had something on his mind. Now all she had to do was let him know she was here if he wanted to talk and try to prevent anymore kissing episodes from happening.

Because kissing Colin had turned into another one of those fantasies leaving her wanting more. But Darcy was a realist by default. She may want a man to love her and a family to go right along with him in her perfect world, or the image she had of perfection, but the truth was Colin and Iris were out of reach.

Darcy had to keep reminding herself of that or she'd be severely crushed when time came to leave…alone.

* * *

Oh. My.

There was a reason Darcy had made her way through the house searching for Colin, but right at this moment she had no clue what it was. In fact, she had no thoughts whatsoever because her mind and her sight were filled with a glorious image of Colin doing one-armed pull-ups, shirtless, displaying that tattoo in a sweaty way that had her all but panting.

Dark skin wrapped around taut muscles flexing with each movement had Darcy gripping the doorframe. She wasn't about to interrupt this free show. There was no way she could miss the chance to see her boss in all his sexy glory. She wasn't dead, after all. She just couldn't think clearly when he was around…an issue she'd never had with any other man.

With a grunt, he pulled himself up one last time before dropping back to the floor. Hands resting on his hips just above his low-slung shorts, Colin's shoulders shifted up and down as he pulled in deep breaths. Then he stilled, turned his head over his shoulder and spotted her.

Busted.

He held her gaze. It was now or never.

"We need to talk," she informed him, bolstering her courage by tamping down her girlie parts and stepping into the gym.

"If you want to work out, fine. I'm not in the mood to talk."

Darcy crossed her arms over her chest. "Seems like your mood is flat-out grouchy."

Colin turned fully to face her, but continued to stare. Darcy wondered if she'd crossed a line. But, boss or not, he shouldn't take his attitude out on her.

"I came to see if you wanted to talk about whatever has you brooding," she went on, trying her hardest to keep her eyes on his and not on the sweaty pecs and the ink that had her heart racing. "This tension is something I prefer not to work around and it's not good for a child because they can sense such things even at an early age."

Colin took a step forward, eyes locked on hers. "Is that right?"

Swallowing, Darcy nodded. "Yes."

He took another step, then another, eventually closing the gap between them. Darcy inhaled that musky, male scent, took in those muscles that were within striking distance and blinked up at Colin.

"If you're trying to intimidate me, you'll have to try harder." She had to keep the upper hand here because her control was slowly slipping and she had to at least put up a strong front. "If you don't want to talk, I'll leave you to your workout so you can take out your frustrations that way."

His stunning blue eyes traveled over her face. "Go change and join me."

"I don't think that's a good idea."

"Because of my mood?"

Darcy took in a deep breath. "Among other things."

"Like the pull between us?"

Why deny the obvious? She'd never been one to play games, though she did do her best to avoid uncomfortable situations. So how did she find herself here?

"Whatever has made you all surly is the main issue," she stated. "But the attraction is something we already discussed and agreed to ignore."

The muscle in Colin's jaw ticked, his nostrils flared. "Discussing and ignoring our chemistry isn't going to make it go away. As far as my mood goes, I had a disagreement with my brother on the phone and I'm dealing with some family things. That's all you need to know and more than you're entitled to."

Shaking her head, Darcy took a step back. "Obviously it was a mistake to come down here."

She turned, set on heading up to her room and figuring out new recipes for the coming week. She'd barely taken a step out the door before one strong hand wrapped around her arm and pulled her to a stop.

"The mistake would be leaving."

His words washed over her, his breath tickled the side of her neck, the heat from his body enveloped her. Darcy closed her eyes.

"Colin," she whispered. "I can only be here for Iris. Nothing more."

"You deny yourself too much." His thumb stroked over her bare arm. "The car, new clothes… my touch. I've tried to ignore the power you have over me. I've tried, but there's only so much a man can take. You're driving me crazy and I'm taking my frustrations out on you when it's my fault I can't deal with how much you get under my skin. I snapped at you earlier because I'm angry with myself."

Darcy gasped at his raw honesty.

"Tell me you don't want me to touch you," he whispered.

"I'm not a liar," she informed him. "But I can't let you. There's a difference."

Colin turned her around so fast she fell against him. Instantly, her hands came up to settle on that hard chest she'd been lusting after. Why did she have to have such strong feelings for this man? And why was he so forceful, so dominating and constantly arousing at every single moment of the day?

"Being alone with you is not a good idea." Her defense came out weak, and the smirk on his face told her he wasn't buying it, either. "I need this job, Colin. I can't afford to…well…whatever you have in mind."

With a low growl from deep in his throat, Colin framed her face with both hands, forcing her to look only at him.

"*Moro*, you have no idea what I have in mind."

Moro. What did that even mean? Something

Greek, she assumed. Coming from his lips, though, it sounded sexy, naughty.

No, she didn't want to appreciate the seductive terms rolling off his tongue, dripping with a toe-curling accent.

With taut skin beneath her palms, Darcy was fighting the urge to dig her fingers into his heated skin, rise on her toes and take what he was so blatantly offering.

"This isn't professional." She focused on his face, wondering if he was having doubts, but all she saw staring back at her was desire.

Had a man ever looked at her in such an arousing way before? If she had to ask herself the question, the obvious answer was no.

"No, it's not," he agreed, still holding her face in his hands. "But damn it, the more I fight this, the more I crave it. Do you want to quit working for me?"

"No."

"I'm not about to fire you." His thumb stroked over her bottom lip, back and forth. "So that leaves us here, fighting an urge that's only gaining momentum. What do you want?"

Was he mocking her? What did he think she

wanted to do? She wanted this ache to cease, but she didn't want to be so clichéd as to sleep with her boss.

"I think you need to keep your hands off me," she whispered. "I think we need to focus on Iris and I think we need to be adult enough to have self-control."

Colin slid his hands back through her hair, tipped her head up and inched even closer, leaving only a breath between their mouths.

"I didn't ask what you thought. I asked what you want."

With her hands trapped between their bodies, his firm grip on her and air barely passing between them, Darcy did the only thing she could think to do…she kissed him.

Instantly Colin took control, pushing her back against the wall. Her hands fell away and just as she tried to grip his shoulders, he grabbed her wrists, jerked them away from his body and had both arms pinned up over her head. She was at his total mercy, at his command. His mouth covered hers, dominated, possessed and every part of her wanted more, wanted him.

Her body arched into his. The sensation of

those hard planes against her had any feeling of self-consciousness disappearing. Apparently Colin didn't seem to mind his woman a little on the curvy side. If his arousal was any indication, he actually preferred a little extra flesh.

With one hand gripping her wrists, Colin's other hand found the hem of her shirt. His fingers slid beneath the cotton and found her waist. His palm flattened against her heated skin as he brushed his thumb along the satiny barrier of her bra. Such a thin layer, yet it proved to be quite a hindrance. She wanted his hands on her, all over her.

Darcy groaned as his hips pushed against hers; his thumb glided back and forth over her breast. He utterly consumed her with the simplest yet most demanding of touches and she still burned for more.

Wait. What was she saying? He was a widower. He'd been married and his wife had passed not too long ago. So, what did that make Darcy? The rebound? A fling to help him recover from a broken heart?

Wasn't that precisely what Colin was to her? Hadn't her own heart—and apparently her common sense, too—taken a hit from her failed relationship? Were they using each other as stepping-stones to get beyond the hurt?

With her arms still locked above her head by Colin's firm grip, Darcy tore her mouth away, causing his lips to land on her jawline.

"Colin," she panted. "Wait…just…this is…stop. Please."

He froze. His hand fell from her shirt as he slowly backed away. The second he released her arms, Darcy pulled some much needed air into her lungs.

With a curse, Colin raked a hand through his damp hair and turned away. Darcy watched as he walked over and sank onto the weight bench, rested his elbows on his knees and dropped his head between his shoulders. Apparently he was at war with himself.

Unsure of what to do next, Darcy remained still, hoping he'd say something to cut through this instant strain that settled between them. "Go upstairs, Darcy."

The angst in his tone had her glued to the spot. He may want to be alone, but she didn't think he should be. How could she just walk out after what they'd experienced? Ignoring it would only create more friction.

"I'll go," she informed him, smoothing her hair away from her face. "But you need to know something first."

Darcy risked walking toward him and rounding the bench to talk face-to-face, even though he still kept his focus on the ground between his legs.

"I won't be used as someone to pass the time and I won't be anyone's rebound. Yes, I'm attracted to you, but I can work and put that aside." Pulling in a deep breath of air and straightening her shoulders, she pushed forward. "What I can't do is get wrapped up in an affair that will leave me wanting more because I've been hurt before. I'm not going to lie, I'm still recovering from that betrayal. Right now I have to look out for myself because I have no one else. And as much as I'd like to take you up on what you were offering, I can't sacrifice my heart. I'm not a fling type of girl and I know what might be temporary pleasure to you would be much more than I can handle."

Slowly, Colin lifted his head, sought her gaze

and nodded. "I won't touch you again. I won't kiss you and I'll make sure not to put you in a position where we're alone. Iris will be our focus. I have enough going on in my life without adding more complications."

Darcy fisted her hands at her sides. This is what she wanted him to say, right? She wanted him to treat her as a professional and not make her choose between her morals and her desires.

Yet now that he'd pulled up this invisible wall between them, Darcy couldn't help but wonder if she'd just be on the outside looking in at what she could've had. And this incident confirmed he was looking for an emotional crutch. Trouble was, she was, too, and hadn't even realized it.

Colin came to his feet, keeping his intense gaze on her. "You need to know that I never meant to make you feel like you were passing my time. I haven't been this attracted to a woman in years and damn if this timing isn't inconvenient. You're my nanny, for pity's sake. But I need to clarify one thing before you go upstairs and we table this discussion."

Darcy swallowed. "What?"

Softly, gently, Colin eased forward and touched

his lips to hers for the briefest of moments before easing back. He touched her nowhere else, but just that simple kiss packed as much of a punch as when he'd practically taken her standing up.

"You deserve more than a fling, more than a quickie against the wall." His whispered tone washed over her. "There are just some promises I can't make."

Sliding her tongue over her bottom lip, she savored him. "Why did you kiss me again?"

Bright cobalt eyes locked her in place. "Because I'm selfish and I wanted one last taste."

Heart in her throat, Darcy resisted the urge to reach up and touch her tingling lips. He'd told her he had nothing else to give but a fling and she refused to settle for a few moments of pleasure. She was worth more than that and she'd promised herself after Thad left her with nothing that she wouldn't succumb to passion and charming men again.

On shaky legs, Darcy skirted around Colin and headed out of the gym. By the time she hit the steps, she was nearly running.

What would tomorrow bring, she wondered as she closed herself into her suite. Could they truly put every kiss, every touch behind them? Could she forget the fact she'd felt proof of his desire for her? That he'd touched her breast? They'd crossed into another level of intimacy and that wasn't something Darcy took lightly.

She was just about to change into her pajamas when a piercing cry came from the monitor.

Duty called. She only hoped duty wasn't calling up Colin, as well.

Eight

"How's the nanny working out?"

Colin cringed at his brother's question. For the past three days he'd managed to keep his promise to always have Iris present if he was in the room with Darcy. On the night he'd all but consumed Darcy, right after she had left the gym and Iris had started to cry, Colin had made his way upstairs and waited for a moment to make sure Darcy went into the nursery to care for his little girl.

Being so close, inhaling her fruity scent, seeing her handle Iris in such a loving, caring way, had had him questioning his sanity. They still had months to go and he was no closer to controlling his hormones than he was the moment he opened his door to her. But how could he kick her out when she and Iris were obviously the perfect pairing?

"That good, huh?" Stefan chuckled.

Colin gripped the phone, hating how his brother was across the globe and could still hone in on the truth.

"She's amazing with Iris," Colin stated. "I'm surprised how fast she's has taken to Darcy. Most times Iris prefers Darcy over me when we're playing a game. She climbs into her lap. It's like she's already choosing sides."

"And how have you taken to Darcy?" Stefan asked.

"She's the nanny. That's all."

Stefan's mocking chuckle filled the line. "Pretty defensive. I admit, I'm happy to hear it. I worried about you after Karina's death and then the backlash and speculation from the media. You closed in on yourself for a bit, but with this nanny, you sound a bit…agitated. You're showing signs of life again. You must like her on more than a professional level."

Colin watched out his office window as Darcy and Iris splashed around in the pool. Why did he torture himself by standing in here staring at her? Why did her faded, plain black one-piece do ridiculous things to his libido?

"That doesn't mean anything is going on with my nanny," he grumbled. Maybe he was so moody because nothing *was* going on with the nanny.

Darcy lifted Iris into her arms and climbed from the pool. With each step up, water sluiced off Darcy's curvy body. Watching as she bent to retrieve Iris's towel was pure hell. For several moments Colin took note of how Darcy cared for Iris, drying her off and making sure she was warm before focusing on herself.

And those few minutes were more than enough to have his body responding. He never should've gone so far the other night because now when he saw her, he could actually *feel* her. The combination was killing him.

"The ball is less than two weeks away," Stefan went on, oblivious to Colin's state. "If you're not here, the media will only try to crucify you more. Even though they won't be inside, they'll be hovering outside the palace to see who's here. Besides, word will get out and rumors will fly."

"I'm well aware of how the media would handle my absence."

Colin turned from the window. The last thing he wanted to think about was returning to Galini Isle for a ball hosting the monarchies from surrounding countries. The only bright light was that his best friend, Luc, would be in attendance, and since the man had recently gotten engaged Colin wanted to congratulate the happy couple in person.

But right now he wanted to forget all duties, all pressing issues that demanded his attention. Still, if he didn't go, Stefan was right, it would be like throwing gasoline on the proverbial fire. He just wished he weren't so confused. He was happy here, albeit sexually frustrated. He enjoyed living in California, but he also missed his brother. And being away from his duties had Colin wondering what his late parents would've thought of his actions. Would they support his decision if he chose to walk away? Would they be disappointed?

If he ended up going to the ball, he'd have to

reveal his true identity to Darcy. Traveling back for the event would be tiring and he'd want her with him to help with Iris. A small sliver of him wanted her to know, he wanted to see how she'd treat him if she knew the truth. He liked to think she'd still be the same Darcy he'd come to respect and desire.

"I'll let you know what I decide," Colin stated as he headed down the hall and upstairs to his bedroom. "I'll give you a few days' notice for security."

"They're already on standby," Stefan confirmed. "They're ready to come to LA and hover over you. I had to tell them to stand down more than once."

"Keeping my identity a secret would be kind of hard with royal guards surrounding the perimeter of my home."

"Which is why I'm honoring your wishes and letting you have some privacy. But you'll have to make some decisions soon and I'm not just referring to the ball."

Colin closed his bedroom door and toed off his shoes. "You'll be the first to know what I decide. Right now I have more pressing matters to deal with."

Stefan chuckled. "I'm sure you do."

Colin disconnected the call, cutting off Stefan's mocking laugh. Quickly changing his clothes, Colin decided he was taking charge of everything in his personal life starting now. He was torn up over the decision involving his royal status, but he refused to have his libido all out of control, too. He was going to take what he wanted…and he wanted Darcy Cooper.

How would he know if whatever they were feeling was something real? Colin had told her he couldn't give her more, but those words had been spoken out of fear. He didn't want her to think he was using her, but he ached for her in ways he hadn't known possible.

Lust was something he remembered from his bachelor days, but Darcy was worth more than that shallow emotion and damn if it wasn't complicating everything right now.

He'd given her the space he promised. He'd watched her, kept his hands to himself and had not made any innuendos whatsoever. His self-control was choking him to death.

Their connection was obvious. Why couldn't they spend these next few months enjoying each other? Surely by the time he was ready to move on they'd be tired of each other.

Seduction would be the key to winning her over and he had every intention of pulling out all stops and making her just as achy and needy as he was. This entire plan was a risk because he knew he wanted to explore more, but what would happen if they reached the point of no return?

Iris wasn't acting sleepy at all after the swim and brief snack, so Darcy slipped back into the pool. Schedules were important for babies, but so was soaking up all the fun and memories they could. Delaying Iris's nap by half an hour wouldn't hurt. The other day the nap had been put off for too long, hence the mega tantrum, but Darcy had learned what Iris's nap meltdown threshold was.

Easing Iris into her baby raft with canopy, Darcy held onto the side and swished the float around in the water. Iris squealed and clapped her hands with each twist. Her little legs were working back and forth beneath the water.

Darcy couldn't help but laugh as an immeasurable amount of joy filled her heart. There truly was nothing like a baby's sweet laugh. Darcy watched Iris's face as she led her further into the pool. Those bright eyes really sparkled in the sunlight…and reminded Darcy how much Iris looked like her daddy.

Dunking down lower to get her shoulders wet, Darcy tried her hardest to keep images of Colin from her mind. Of course the harder she fought, the more he kept creeping into her thoughts. It was so, so difficult to keep her professional feelings separate from her personal ones.

Darcy loved Iris, enjoyed every moment she got to spend with her. But she also thoroughly enjoyed Colin's company on a level that she hadn't expected. Her mind and her heart were in agreement for once, telling her that feeling anything for the man was a bad idea.

A flash of him doing chin-ups with one muscular arm, the memory of how he'd stared so intently into her eyes the instant before he claimed her mouth flooded her thoughts. Then there was the other side of him that also played through her mind. The man was an amazing father, always wanting to give Iris her bath, wanting to spend so much time alone with his little girl. The smile he gave Iris was unlike anything Darcy had ever seen. The man was truly in love with his daughter.

How could Darcy not be attracted to all facets of Colin? He may still be quite mysterious, and he still had that expensive SUV in the drive waiting for her to drive it, but he had her so torn up, she had no choice but to want to know more.

For the past three days he'd stayed away from her unless they were with Iris. Part of her hated the barrier she'd placed between them, but the other part knew the separation was the best thing for her. Between focusing on her business and reminding herself she needed to guard her heart, Darcy couldn't afford to fall into a fling no matter how she desired to do just that.

Memories of how amazing his weight had felt pressed against her as his mouth consumed her would just have to suffice. Unfortunately, right now, all the memories were doing was leaving her achier.

"How can I stay inside and work when there's so much fun going on out here?"

Darcy froze the same instant Iris squealed for her daddy.

No. No. No. She didn't want to turn around because if she did she knew she'd see Colin wearing some type of swimming trunks that only showcased his impressive set of abs and all of his other magnificent muscles.

She wanted to hide, to instantly be poolside and wrapped in a towel so he didn't have to see her get out of the water with her thighs jiggling and her rounded stomach that had stretched her "miracle suit" beyond the promised miracle.

From the corner of her eye, Darcy spotted a flash of black just as Colin dove headfirst into the pool. What was he thinking coming out here with her? Yes, Iris was present as they'd discussed, but he wasn't naive. He knew exactly what coming out here half naked would do to her. What type of game was he playing?

When Colin surfaced, much closer to her than she'd anticipated, he swiped the water back from his forehead and smiled at Iris.

"Hey, baby. Are you having fun?"

With Colin's hands on the raft, Darcy eased back. No way was she going to accidentally entangle her legs with his because she'd quite possibly start to whimper, which would completely override the speech she'd given him three days ago.

"I'll just let you two have some time alone."

Darcy made her way to the steps. There was no good way to get out without Colin seeing her ancient, threadbare suit pasted against every dip and roll. Best to just get out, fake a confidence she didn't own and run like hell for the nearest towel.

"You don't have to get out because I'm here."

Darcy knew full well the man had his eyes on her, but she didn't turn to meet his gaze until she was properly wrapped like a terrycloth sausage.

"I'm not," she told him, lying through her smile.

Colin adjusted the canopy over Iris to keep her shaded. "Are you going to run every time you get uncomfortable?"

Gripping her towel at her breasts, Darcy straightened her shoulders. "I'm not running."

"But you're uncomfortable," he said with a smirk. "Your rules, Darcy. You can cancel them at any time and take what we both want for as long as we're here."

No, she couldn't.

"She'll need a nap soon," Darcy told him, dodging the obvious topic. "Just bring her in and I'll get her all dried off and ready. If you don't object, I plan on making almond-crusted chicken and grilled veggies for dinner."

"No objections here. At least not on dinner."

The man was so confusing. One minute he was moody and kissing her so she had to put on the brakes. The next minute he was agreeing to her terms and then he tried to muddle her mind by flashing that chest that should be enshrined in gold.

Darcy marched into the house, not in the mood to play whatever game he was offering. He had issues of his own, at least he said he did, and so did she. They had a temporary working relationship. Pursuing anything beyond that agreement would be wrong and settle so much awkwardness between them they'd never find their way out.

The last time she'd fallen hard for a man, she'd let him into her life, into her business because her grandmother thought he was perfect for Darcy. Darcy had trusted her hormones and ignored common sense for too long.

She'd let business and pleasure mix once before and she'd be paying for that mistake for the
rest of her life.

Nine

Darcy may want him to give up, but until he quit seeing desire in her eyes each time she looked at him, he wasn't backing down. She'd been burned before and now Colin was paying for another man's sins.

She may have asked for space, and he wasn't one to go against a woman's wishes, but that didn't mean he still couldn't get what he wanted.

True, the house was huge so giving her space wasn't necessarily a problem. But their physical connection was so intense that the walls seemed to close in on them.

At first he'd fought the attraction, then he'd resigned himself to the fact it wasn't going away.

Then he'd wondered if they could both heal by seeking comfort in each other. But as that thought ran through his mind, he couldn't help but wonder if there was something more building here.

He sounded like a woman thinking through all of his feelings and emotions, but Darcy was bringing out a side he hadn't known existed and he didn't want to cheapen whatever this was to a potential fling. They both deserved more than that, yet he couldn't help but want her and there was no point in trying to fight the tension anymore.

He'd failed in his attempt at seduction at the pool earlier today. He thought for sure spending time with her in a more relaxed setting with Iris would soften her. Now Darcy was up in her room and he was once again in the gym. He couldn't even come into this room anymore without seeing her pressed against the wall, flushed from arousal and looking up at him beneath heavy lids.

There had to be a way to break down the barrier she'd encompassed herself in. There were so many layers he'd yet to peel away. He wanted to know why she only wore three outfits and rotated them. He wanted to know why she was sewing things in her spare time and why she sneaked down to the gym early in the mornings before Iris woke when she thought he was still asleep. On a rare occasion he would catch her searching the internet for more recipes. Seems that cooking wasn't just a fun hobby for her as she'd stated, but a true passion.

Still, she'd made it apparent she didn't want to be alone with him so talking to her was damn near impossible, because when Iris was around he wanted to devote his time and attention to his daughter.

Colin pushed the bar back into locked position and sat up on the bench. Swiping a hand across his forehead, he cleared away the sweat as a brilliant plan entered his mind. He was going to have to get creative, to make sure there was no way she could run from what was happening between them. And something was happening whether she wanted to admit it or not.

Sliding his cell from his shorts pocket, Colin quickly did a search for the number he'd used when he'd first contacted her and placed the call. "Colin?" she answered, confusion lacing her tone.

He chuckled. "Yeah."

"Why are you calling my cell?"

A nugget of doubt slid through his mind, but he pressed on because he'd never backed away from a challenge.

"To talk."

Silence settled over the line. Maybe this was a mistake, but it was a risk he was willing to take. Hadn't he always been a daredevil? Hence his accident and recovery. "Darcy?"

"I'm here." She let out a sigh and a faint sound of sheets rustling filtered through the line. "What do you want to talk about? We're in the same house. You *are* in the house, right?"

He came to his feet and reached for a towel hanging over a weight machine. "I'm in the gym." Colin mopped off his face and neck, and flung the towel into the bin in the corner. "Did I wake you?"

"No. I had just turned off my light and crawled into bed."

Closing his eyes, he could easily picture her spread out on his guest bed, her dark, rich hair spilling over the crisp, white sheets. What did she wear to bed? A T-shirt? Something silky, perhaps? Nothing?

"Is everything okay?" she asked. "I'm a little confused as to why you're calling me."

"I want to hear your voice."

Colin shut off the light in the gym and headed toward his office. Only a small desk lamp lit the room. He knew he had to keep control of this conversation or she'd hang up.

"Tell me about your life before you came here."

Darcy laughed. "What about it? I work with kids and love to cook—that's about as exciting as I am."

She was so much more and he'd be the man to show her. Whoever she'd been with last was a jerk who hadn't realized what a treasure he had.

"You have friends, yes?" he asked.

"Yes. I was living with my best friend before I came here. What about you? You're from Greece, you're an amazing father, you keep simple working hours, but that's all I know."

"I'm not talking about me." He sank onto the leather sofa, leaned back and shut his eyes. He wanted to hear all about her, wanted her sultry, sleepy voice to wash over him. "We're talking about you."

"This Q and A can go both ways," she replied with a hint of a challenge. "How about we take turns? I'll go first. Why are you still trying to seduce me?"

"Wow. You sure you don't want to lead in with something lighter? My favorite color is red and my favorite sport is rock climbing."

"You're dodging the question," she stated. "You are the one who started this game."

"Fine. I want you." He shifted on the couch and propped his feet up on the cushions, then leaned back on the arm. "Why are you afraid to be alone with me?"

"Because you're sneaky and I wouldn't be able to resist you."

Colin smiled, settling a hand on his bare abs. "I'm not sneaky, I'm honest."

"That's debatable." She sighed and Colin imagined her upstairs in the dark, aching for him as much as he was for her. "It's my turn. How did you injure yourself?"

"I was rock climbing and made an error in judgment. Trusted the wrong rock."

Darcy's gasp had his own gut clenching. He was actually glad for the head trauma because he didn't remember the fall in any way. A minor blessing.

"You could've been killed," she cried.

"I nearly was. The doctors weren't so sure at first, but once they knew I would live, they told my wife I would never walk again."

"You're remarkable," she whispered.

As much as his ego loved her stroking it, Colin really didn't want her pity because of his accident. He wanted her, no question. But he understood she was burned in the past and he knew she was struggling for money, so she definitely had more at stake than he did.

"Tell me about the jerk who broke your heart."

Darcy groaned. "Why don't you ask something else?"

"Because my backup question is me wanting to know how fast I can be in your room with nothing between us but the darkness."

"You're not playing fair," she muttered.

Colin gritted his teeth. "Baby, I'm not playing at all. I'm tired of playing. We've danced around this attraction for too long and I'm going insane."

"Fine. We'll discuss the ex."

He didn't know if he wanted to laugh or cry at the reply.

Darcy's deep inhale had Colin eagerly waiting, but knowing he'd probably want to hunt this guy down and make him pay. Colin had no reason to be jealous, no reason to be so territorial... yet he was.

"My ex took every single dime I had to my name. I trusted him with more than my heart, he was my new business partner after my grandmother passed, and he betrayed me. Apparently he had another girlfriend and was using my money to buy her presents. And by presents I mean trips, a car, a condo." Darcy paused and Colin wasn't sure if there was more or if she was waiting for him to reply. After another soft sigh, she continued. "He not only ruined my business, he killed my dream of adopting a child."

Colin tamped down his anger. Whoever this bastard was, Colin loathed the man and wished for about five minutes alone with him. The fact he'd stolen all of her money was a sin in itself, but to know Darcy wanted to adopt was a morsel of information he was shocked she'd revealed.

Did she have a dream of adopting because she was compassionate toward kids and wanted to save them? Did she not plan on marrying? Or was there something medical that prevented her from having her own?

She'd answered one question and triggered a multitude of others.

But now he realized why Darcy had so little with her, why she was so upset over the new car and him having hers taken away without asking first. Her ex had thrown money around, albeit hers, and had used the funds to further his own desires. This woman was a fighter and she wasn't about to take handouts from the likes of Colin. How could he not admire how strong-willed she was?

Fortunately, he'd gotten her car back, now fixed, and it sat in one of the bays of his second garage behind the house. But even though he'd smoothed things over with Darcy, Colin didn't want to stop there. He was already in deep with her, so why not keep going to satisfy his curiosity?

"What's his name?" Colin asked.

"I'm sorry?"

Colin fisted his hand over his abs. "The lowlife who stole from you. I want his name."

"It's not your turn."

Her tone left no room for argument, so he waited for her to ask her question.

"You're a man of mystery. What's your profession?"

"I'm a CEO of sorts." Okay, there was no good way to answer, but he was a leader…for now. "I manage a large group back in Greece."

There. That sounded believable, didn't it? It was his turn to ask a question, but he wasn't wasting it on her ex's name. He could find that out later and take care of things. Right now, he wanted to dig deeper, to get to the point of his call. Priorities.

"What are you wearing?" he asked.

Darcy's soft laugh enveloped him as if she stood before him. Damn, he wanted to touch her, to kiss her, to feel her beneath him. He'd only known her several weeks and she all but consumed him. Obviously she had no clue the power she held over him.

"Are we playing that game now?" she all but

mocked. "I'm wearing a black, silky chemise that leaves very little to the imagination."

Colin swallowed, the image now burned in his mind. "You're lying."

"You'll never know. What are you wearing?"

"Shorts and sweat. I just finished my workout where all I could do was see you pinned against the wall with your eyes closed, your mouth on mine and my hand up your shirt."

Darcy sighed. "What are you doing to me?" she whispered. "I can't keep up with how quick you turn me inside out."

"That goes both ways, *erastis*."

"What does that mean?"

"Come down to my office and I'll tell you." More like show her.

"I can't, Colin. You're making this so difficult for me. You have to understand that just because I want something, doesn't mean I can take it. Apparently you're used to getting what you want."

"I always get what I want."

"Sounds like a threat."

Colin smiled. "It's a promise."

"Tell me about your wife."

Colin eased up and shook his head. No way was

he getting into how he'd let his wife down when he'd lived his reckless lifestyle and then pushed her away when he'd truly needed her most. He totally took the blame for their failed marriage because he'd been too proud, too stubborn to let her just help him through his rough time. Which was beyond ironic since he'd hired Darcy to assist him because he'd finally come to the realization he couldn't do it all.

Maybe it was time to break the cycle. To finally let someone in and keep his stubborn pride on the back burner. But, right now he had other, more pressing matters.

"Let's table that discussion for another time."

"Count on it," she said around a yawn.

"I'll let you go," he told her. "I need to hit the shower before I head to bed."

"I'll just be lying here in my chemise, dreaming."

Colin fisted his hand and came to his feet. "You're getting too good at this. Better watch what you say, you're playing with fire."

"You lit the match."

When she hung up, Colin stood in his office with a painful arousal and a ridiculous grin on his face. Yeah, he was used to getting what he wanted and he wanted Darcy in his bed.

And he would have her there. It was only a matter of time.

Darcy hadn't slept at all. Once Colin had started with the "what are you wearing" game her mind had formed so many fantasies, leaving her restless and aroused.

She hadn't lied when she said she was lying in her bed wearing a black chemise. She actually owned two. Sleeping in something so soft, so flawless gliding over her skin always made her feel more feminine. After dealing with children all day and spending most of her waking hours dealing with various problems and parents, she had to stay in touch with her femininity even if she wasn't sleeping with anyone.

Which was why last night's little chat with Colin left her aching in ways she'd never thought possible. She'd been with one man, and even during their intimacy Darcy had never felt an inkling of what she'd felt last night on the phone with Colin.

The man wasn't just chipping away at the defensive wall she'd erected, he was blasting through it with a sledgehammer. He'd started opening up just a touch over the past several weeks and he'd become playful, flirty and flat-out blatant regarding what he wanted.

Because she hadn't slept very well, she was awake even earlier than usual and in the gym. Of course, during her entire workout all she could picture was Colin down here last night. How long had he been sweating and working out while thinking of her? Did he regret calling her? Had he assumed she'd come running to him and they'd enter into this affair without giving the consequences another thought?

When she glanced at the time on her phone, she realized she'd been working out for over an hour. A great improvement over the first day. Granted, she'd had a hard time concentrating with Colin flexing his perfectly honed muscles all over the place.

If she could keep up this regime while she was here and continue eating healthily, she just may be on the fast track to getting her life back. In such a short time she already felt better about herself and had more energy.

More energy was something she would most definitely need if she was going to continue to battle Colin and his bold advances.

Darcy headed back upstairs, careful as always to be quiet while Iris and Colin slept. Grabbing a quick shower would give her time to get her thoughts in order before facing Colin. She knew the mutual desire would not go away. And as if fighting her urges wasn't enough, he wasn't playing fair. How could she keep putting up a strong front when he'd pretty much laid his cards on the table?

Lathering up her hair, she slid the strands through her fingers beneath the spray. She'd been worried about getting entangled with Colin after her last romance debacle, but Colin was so different from her ex. She only had to look at his interactions with Iris to see how loving he was. And he wasn't out to use her for anything because at this point he knew she had nothing to give.

Maybe he wanted her for no other reason than to satisfy his curiosity…just as she felt with him.

Darcy rinsed her body and shut off the water. Quickly she toweled off. She'd just pulled her hair into a messy topknot when fussy noises blared through the monitors.

Iris was crankier in the mornings than any other baby she'd dealt with. Of course, Darcy hadn't personally worked with a vast number of children under two, but Iris was certainly special. The toddler was happiest when she got her food. Darcy could totally relate.

Darcy wrestled her sports bra back on and yanked up her shorts; she didn't have time to find something else. When she turned the corner of her room and hit the doorway of the nursery, Colin was lifting Iris from her crib. That toned back with ink scrolling over his shoulder continued to mock her, because every time she saw it, she wanted to trace it…with her tongue.

The way he gently spoke to Iris, the way he held such a delicate little girl against his hard, strong body really hit Darcy. Even rumpled from sleep, Colin Alexander was a man who demanded attention without saying a word.

When he turned and caught her gaze, his eyes did some evaluating of their own. Darcy was reminded she stood before him in only her sweaty sports bra and shorts. Not her best look, considering she wasn't perfectly proportioned or toned in any way.

"I just got out of the shower and threw on the closest thing," Darcy stated, keeping her eyes locked on Colin as he continued to close the gap between them. "Give me one minute to change and I can take her and feed her."

Colin's limp was a bit more pronounced this morning. Most likely he'd slept wrong. How had the man slept after that call? Maybe she was more revved up with this sexual tension than he was.

"You're flushed." His eyes traveled to the scoop in her bra and back up. "Looks good on you."

"Colin—"

"Go change," he urged. "I'll feed Iris and you better be fully dressed next time you're around me."

Darcy stared at him for another minute, which was a minute too long because he reached out, trailed a fingertip across her collarbone.

"Go, *erastis,* before I take what I want."

That was the second time he'd called her that and she wanted to know what it meant. She had a feeling it was a term of endearment or something sexy because his voice took on a whole other tone when he said it. She was drowning where this man was concerned and she knew it was just a matter of time before she succumbed to all of the desire and passion that kept swirling around them.

Darcy turned and all but ran into her adjoining bath. The man was killing her. She dug out a pair of jeans and her favorite pink T-shirt before heading back downstairs, praying she'd have control over her emotions. She should be praying Colin would have control over his.

She didn't see them in the kitchen, but the sound of the patio doors sliding open drew her attention. Through the wide window she spotted Colin with a banana in one hand and Iris holding onto the other as he led her out onto the stone patio. He'd just placed her on the settee when he lost his balance and went down. Darcy ran out the door and was crouched at his side in an instant.

Had he reinjured himself? Worry flooded her. How she would get him back up without hurting him further?

With a muttered curse in his native tongue, Colin pushed her away. "Don't. Just take her inside and feed her."

Darcy reached for him. "Let me help you up."

"Leave me be," he shouted, meeting and holding her gaze. "I'm not paying you to coddle me, I'm paying you to care for Iris."

Darcy jerked back and came to her feet. Iris started to climb off the chair and Darcy reached down, taking the little girl's hand.

"You're right," Darcy replied, swallowing the hurt. "I'll remember my place from now on."

Colin shifted and stood, wincing as he did so. Even though his jab sliced deep, Darcy waited until he got his bearings. Just as he opened his mouth to speak, Darcy turned.

"Come on, baby girl." Darcy swiped the banana from the ground where Colin had dropped it when he fell. "Let's get you some breakfast."

No way would Darcy make the mistake of trying to get close and help Colin again. If he wanted to run hot and cold with his emotions, he could do so with someone else. Darcy wasn't here as an outlet for his frustrations and anger over his accident.

Ten

Disgrace was a bitter, nasty pill to swallow.

After his spill that morning, Colin didn't know what he was angrier about, himself for falling and possibly hurting Iris or the fact that Darcy was there to witness his humiliation. He'd taken his anger and embarrassment out on her for no reason.

Hadn't he hired a nanny in case something like this happened? The real possibility that he would fall in the presence of, or God forbid, while holding Iris, had been his main concern. What he hadn't planned on was having his hormones thrown into the mix. And he hadn't been forthcoming with Darcy about his injury because he'd prayed there wouldn't be a mishap while she was here. He didn't want to be seen as weak or crippled.

Colin sneaked into the house through the back door after Darcy had taken Iris in for breakfast. After he'd showered and gotten his damn leg and back under control with some stretches his doctor and therapist had shown him, Colin felt somewhat human again.

This morning his goal had been to carry on the plan of seduction that he'd started on the phone last night. Then his past had come back to bite him when he'd fallen, completely erasing any impact he may have had on Darcy last night because of his inability to handle this entire situation like a mature adult. Wow, wasn't he just the king of all things sexy? Now instead of Darcy viewing him as a strong, confident man, she saw him as a cripple, as someone who couldn't even care for himself, let alone a child.

If the paparazzi back in Galini Isle ever caught a glimpse of his inability to stand on his own two feet at times, he'd be ridiculed, questioned and thrust into the limelight even more. They'd already speculated that he and Karina were falling apart, but since her death, they hadn't left him alone and he was sick of the pity, the way they portrayed him as helpless and lost.

He was an Alexander. They were strong men, determined and focused. Nothing would stand in the way of him getting everything he wanted.

Needing to get back on track and spend time with his daughter, Colin figured today would be a great day for a little outing. Darcy might not like men who threw their weight and money around, but he wanted to treat her. Out of every woman he'd ever known, Darcy most definitely deserved to be pampered, even if only for a few hours.

If she was working for him, then she was going to be treated like royalty.

Which reminded him, he needed to have a serious talk with her. He'd decided to attend the ball and he wanted Darcy to come with him. That conversation would have to take place at just the right time. He didn't want her to feel as if he'd lied to her...though he had by omission.

Just as Colin reached the bottom of the stairs, he heard Darcy's laughter and Iris's sweet giggle. That combination slid a new emotion through him—one he wasn't sure he could identify and one he wasn't sure he wanted to.

When he found them on the floor in the living room, Colin stopped in the wide, arched doorway to take in the scene. Days ago the sight of freshly picked flowers, obviously from the landscaping, all over his floor would've had him enraged. But now, seeing those vibrant petals in Darcy's and Iris's hair had him smiling. These two were like kindred spirits and he could easily get wrapped up in watching them.

There he went again, sliding down that slippery slope even further toward Darcy. He had lost control somewhere between opening the door that first day and the first time she'd verbally matched him with her banter.

"Daddy!"

Iris squealed, scooped up all the flowers her little hands could hold and sprinkled them on top of Darcy's head.

"Deedee pitty," she exclaimed, clapping her hands.

Darcy glanced his way, but quickly darted away. "I'm Deedee. It's much easier for her to say."

Colin hated how Darcy wouldn't even look at him. He'd done that to her when he'd sworn he wouldn't hurt anyone again over this injury. Because of his inexcusable actions, he'd driven a wedge between them.

The fact his daughter had adopted a nickname for Darcy added another layer of bonding that was already wrapped so tightly around them. All part of the nanny-child relationship, nothing more—or at least that's what he needed to keep telling himself. Darcy wasn't part of this family; her presence was temporary.

"Darcy, go get yourself and Iris ready. We're going out for the day." He moved into the room and slid his hand over Iris's dark curls. "I'll work on cleaning this mess up."

Darcy came to her feet, catching the flowers as they fell down her chest. "I'm sorry. We went for a little walk and picked some flowers from the gardens. I planned on cleaning—"

Colin held up a hand, cutting off her words, and offered a smile so she didn't think he was angry or a complete jerk after how he'd treated her earlier. "I've got it. Really. Go on."

"Okay." She bent down, lifted Iris into her arms and turned back to him. Finally, she met his eyes with a worry he didn't want. "Are you feeling all right?"

She didn't come out and ask about the fall, but he knew that's exactly what she was referring to.

He gave her a brief nod. "Do you want to know where we're going?" he asked.

Darcy's lids lowered. "My place isn't to ask questions. You're paying me to care for Iris, so I'm going to get us ready."

Colin absolutely loathed the words he'd spouted off to her earlier out of anger and humiliation. There was no taking them back now that they were out in the open. All he could do was show her he wasn't the ogre she thought he'd become.

Darcy left the room without another word. He needed to apologize, but words would only go so far. He would show her that he wasn't a terrible person. He'd make her see that she didn't have to work her butt off for nothing.

And by the time she left him at the end of her term, she'd never have to worry about her business or her finances again. If he did nothing else, he'd make damn sure of that.

He had to be kidding. That dress—as stunning as it was—cost more than an entire month's worth of groceries. Colin had talked her into shopping, but she'd had no idea he'd pull her into the most expensive store she'd ever seen in her entire life.

After working for him for several weeks now, one would think she'd have the courage to stand her ground and decline.

On the flipside, though, she'd discovered with each passing day that Colin was impossible to resist.

"At least try it on," he urged, holding up the elegant, one-shouldered, bright blue dress.

Darcy wasn't in the mood to be shopping, but Colin had claimed this was just another work incentive and he truly wanted her to have new clothes. After the morning they'd had, she really had no clue why they were here.

"I won't wear that dress," she told him, though she loved it. Being stubborn could go both ways.

On a sigh, he hung the dress back up and inched closer. "I already apologized, but I'll keep saying it until you realize I am honestly sorry for how I reacted. I know you were only trying to help, but my pride usually doesn't allow me to let others come to my rescue."

That she could understand. She, too, had her

pride and he had come and apologized shortly after she'd completely ignored him.

"I just find it convenient you're getting me clothes today and calling them incentives," she shot back, talking quietly so the salesclerk didn't hear. Iris squealed and chewed on the baby doll in her stroller, oblivious to the turmoil.

"I'd planned on this anyway," he told her. "The timing is just wrong. If you're not in the mood, we can do this another day. I figured we could both use a break and to get out and do something fun."

Something fun? What man found shopping fun? Darcy chewed on her bottom lip as she considered how to approach this. She could be childish, the way he had been the other day, or she could accept the olive branch he was extending.

"Fine," she conceded.

With a wide smile, Colin lifted the dress back off the rack. "What size do you need?"

Darcy laughed, gripping the handle on the Cadillac of strollers. "Nice try, buddy. I'm not telling you my size. It's not in the single digits and I doubt that dress will look good on my frame."

His eyes scanned her body. "Your frame looks

fine and you'll never know how it looks if you don't try it on."

Darcy shook her head and turned toward another rack. "Everything in here is so pricey. Why are we even here?"

Colin's hand came around, gripping hers over the handle. Darcy threw a glance over her shoulder and saw he was much closer than she'd thought.

"Pick out whatever you want." He held up a hand when she started to argue. "I'll take Iris to the toy store next door. Text me when you're done. The clerk has my credit card number."

Darcy closed her eyes. "There's nothing I need that will take me that long. Just give me a couple minutes."

"You may not need it, but you deserve it." His thumb stroked over her hand. "I'm not trying to buy you. I'm trying to put a smile on your face, to let you have whatever you want for the entire day. I'd bet my entire savings that you haven't bought anything for yourself for years."

Darcy glanced down to their hands. The contrast between his dark skin and her paleness was minor in comparison to their many differences.

"I'm not sleeping with you."

Colin jerked her around, his fingers digging into her shoulders. "I'm not offering this shopping trip as a bribe, Darcy. You going to bed with me has nothing to do with this. I'm here because I want to give you nice things while you're with me. If you want to leave everything when you go, then do that and I'll donate the clothes to charity. You were told up front you'd be getting bonuses along the way. Don't argue."

"Yet again, does anyone ever tell you no?" she asked.

A smirk flirted around the corners of his mouth. "You're the only one who keeps trying."

On a sigh, Darcy closed her eyes and nodded. "Fine. I'll pick out a couple of things. Seriously, though, we could find a cheaper store."

His eyes traveled over the racks, the displays and mannequins. "Do you not like this store?"

Darcy laughed. "Everything in here is gorgeous. I just think we could find one with smaller numbers on the price tags."

"Don't look at the price tag. Focus on how stunning you'll look, how beautiful you'll feel." Colin's intense gaze lasted a minute longer than she was comfortable with before he moved around her and gripped the stroller. "Take your time. I've got Miss Iris."

Darcy stared at his retreating back. He paused at the counter and spoke to the pretty female employee. Of course she batted her lashes and laughed at whatever Colin said before he slipped out the front door. The man seemed to have that effect on every female.

Colin was way too charming. Not only did he have that devastatingly handsome, sexy arrogance about him, he had a beautiful baby girl. All he had to do was be the loving, doting father he was and women's ovaries started weeping.

The burn in her throat had her swallowing. Colin and Iris were missing the female figure in their lives and Darcy was missing the family she'd always dreamed of having. Yet they could never mesh together because…well, just because.

She was his employee, she had goals of her own and right now she needed to get her business back up and running. Added to that, Colin made it clear he would probably be leaving in a few months to go back to Greece.

Darcy nearly laughed. She'd never have the

chance to set foot on Colin's home turf. If he wanted to treat her like Cinderella today, she would let him. For once she would let someone else take care of her, do something nice for her.

By the time Darcy finished trying on clothes, she had way more in her want pile than in her "no" pile.

"Miss Cooper," the clerk called from the other side of the thick floor-to-ceiling curtain. "I have some shoes pulled and jewelry for you to look at once you're done. Can I get you any other sizes?"

Shoes? Jewelry? When had she ever purchased an entire outfit complete with head-to-toe accessories?

"My sizes are fine," she called back. "I'll be right out."

When Darcy stepped out of the dressing room, she resisted the urge to adjust her simple V-neck T-shirt. She didn't fit in this place and the clothes she'd tried on certainly wouldn't work for her daily activities relating to Iris's care. But if she left with nothing, she knew Colin would drag her somewhere else.

"What can I take to the counter for you?"

Darcy glanced to the perfectly polished clerk

with her carefully applied makeup and elegantly coiffed hair. Darcy glanced back into the dressing room where she'd hung everything up.

"I'll take that blue dress for now," she told the clerk. "I need to think about everything else."

She hated to admit it, but the blue dress did hug her curves and made her feel beautiful. She didn't mind said curves or her figure so much, and with her workout sessions she was actually starting to see a difference in her body. The extra boost of confidence had her smiling.

Colin had liked the dress, so that's what she'd go with for now. And damn if he wasn't right. It had looked good on her, better than she'd ever imagined…not that she'd admit such a revelation to Colin.

"What size shoe are you? I was guessing a seven."

Amazing how the woman was dead-on, but Darcy shook her head. "Oh, I couldn't—"

"Mr. Alexander made me promise to add shoes and any jewelry you wanted to the outfits you chose." A soft smile spread across her face. "He also said not to argue and worry about the cost."

Darcy couldn't help but laugh. Colin thought

he had all his bases covered. Biting her bottom lip, Darcy pondered what she should actually do versus what she wanted to do. She could go ahead and get the things Colin requested. If she didn't wear anything, he could return them and get his money back.

"I should also tell you, he also made me promise you'd leave with no less than three outfits." With her hands clasped in front of her bright pink capris and crisp white shirt, the clerk nodded toward the dress in Darcy's hand. "He also said you weren't leaving without that blue dress, so I'm glad you already chose that one."

Three outfits? The staggering cost of all that would be beyond ridiculous. Outfits, as well as accessories and shoes. What else did Colin have planned for her? Buying clothes and loaning her a brand-new car were both so personal. When he'd initially said bonuses, Darcy had assumed he'd meant the monetary kind. She really should've asked him for specifics, but she'd been too concerned about keeping her job and making it past the trial period.

"To be honest, I don't have a need for fancy clothes," she told the clerk. "I love everything in here, but I'm a nanny and caring for a child doesn't necessarily require bling and stilettos."

The clerk laughed, reached out and patted her arm. "Tell you what, let's look around and I'm sure we can find something to make you both happy. You can still be fashionable and comfortable while caring for that sweet baby."

An hour later the young worker, whom Darcy now knew as Carly, had delivered on her promise. New shorts, basic tops and adorable sandals were neatly wrapped in tissue paper and placed in two large bags…along with that blue dress Darcy would never have a use for. She had drawn the line at jewelry, though. There was no need for earrings or a necklace for Iris to tug on, not to mention Darcy wasn't preparing herself for a fashion show.

She shot Colin a text, telling him she was finished and she'd come to the toy store to meet him. After thanking Carly for all of her help, Darcy headed out the door. So much money spent for two bags worth of clothing, but he'd insisted, and to be honest she'd never let someone splurge on her before. Colin had been adamant he wanted to do this for her and she was done being stubborn.

Perhaps she was being selfish, but life had thrown so much crap at her, it was nice to have someone refreshing waltz into her life. She truly believed he wasn't buying her to get her into bed. If he'd pursued harder at home, she would have caved and they both knew it. Getting new clothes certainly didn't make her want to jump him. No, she'd wanted to do that from the second he'd opened his door and greeted her.

The bright sun warmed her face as soon as she stepped onto the sidewalk. A familiar scream of delight had Darcy turning her attention down the sidewalk to where Iris sat in her stroller, hugging a brand new elephant in one hand and a waving rather large lollipop in the other. Seeing the big, wide smile across her precious face, Darcy didn't know if she'd ever seen Iris happier.

Colin, on the other hand, looked as though he could use a stiff drink. His hair stood on end as if he'd run his fingers through it for the past hour, his lids were heavy and he appeared to be in a daze.

Darcy held back her laugh, but couldn't stop from smiling as he moved closer. "Looks like you had a good time at the toy store."

Colin's eyes snapped to hers as if he'd just realized she stood near him. "Do you know what they have in that place?"

"I'm assuming toys," Darcy stated.

"From floor to ceiling." He continued to stare as if he'd been traumatized. "But it's not just toys. There's candy. Everything lights up or sings or dances to get your attention. It's not even safe to walk through the line to check out. She was reaching for everything. It's like they don't even care about the parents."

Darcy did laugh now. "Surely this wasn't your first trip to a toy store with her."

Colin blinked, raking a hand over his face. "Actually, it was."

The statement shocked Darcy. Perhaps his late wife had always taken Iris toy shopping. Maybe they had another nanny where they'd lived before and she did all of that. Or maybe someone just delivered toys and they hadn't taken Iris to any stores yet.

"Why don't you take these bags and I'll push Iris." She didn't wait for him to answer as she thrust the sacks into his hands. "Let's head home and I'll start dinner. You look like you need to get back to safer territory. We can't have all those plush toys terrorizing you anymore."

Colin glared at her. "Now you're mocking me. We don't need to go home. I just needed to escape that store with my life."

Darcy started pushing Iris down the sidewalk toward the SUV—the one he'd bought for her use. Yes, the man was used to getting what he wanted, in one sneaky way or another.

"I'm not mocking you," she told him. "I'm just stating a fact based on the evidence you presented to me." Colin grunted in response. Darcy smiled as she loaded Iris into the car seat. "What do you say we head over to the park and let Iris play while you recover? Then we can go home and I'll make dinner."

Colin seemed to think about the suggestion before a wide grin spread across his face. "That's a great idea. It's a beautiful day. We might as well spend it outside."

Elation pumped through Darcy. She was seriously having such an amazing day with them and it had nothing to do with her new purchases. Being out with Iris and Colin was just fun and broke up the monotony of being in the house.

Darcy had been so dead set on not letting Colin buy things for her, yet here she was watching him load the new clothes he'd purchased into a vehicle that he'd also bought for her.

She was not a shallow woman and she certainly wasn't hung up on material objects. But, if she was going to be spending months with Colin and Iris, they would be leaving the house at various times and she couldn't very well keep going out in her ratty old clothes. Granted she didn't need thousands of dollars' worth of clothes, either, but she'd lost that fight. She also planned to leave them behind when her term was over because she didn't think it would be fair to keep them… not unless something deeper happened between her and Colin. And at the rate they were edging closer together emotionally, she wondered how they actually would end up at the end of the six-month term.

As they all settled into the car and Darcy climbed in behind the wheel, she realized the main problem. She was getting too comfortable with this family. Not comfortable the way she had on other nanny jobs, but comfortable as in she'd started envisioning this little family as hers.

The thought alone was utterly ridiculous, but she couldn't stop the daydream any more than she could control her hormones around Colin. Everything about this family struck a chord so deep within her, she knew she'd carry them with her for the rest of her life.

Darcy was completely in love with Iris. The little girl could easily melt anyone's heart.

As for Colin...she knew she wasn't in love with the man, but she did have feelings for him. Feelings that had no place in her life or in this professional atmosphere.

Now if she could just keep telling herself that, maybe she'd believe it. But would she stop fantasizing about him?

Eleven

He had become a creature of habit at a young age, due in part to his royal status. Schedules were a normal part of his life and without them, the members of the palace's security team would not have been able to do their jobs efficiently.

And here in the United States he found he was no different. He was in the middle of his nightly workout, which meant he was sweaty, breathing hard and still aching for the woman who lately occupied his every blasted thought.

Today had been amazing and seeing Darcy's face light up was worth the sacrifice. He knew she wasn't easily bought and that was definitely not his intent.

He treated her just as he would any other employee. Colin and his brother were always quick to supply anything the members of their staff needed. Just because he was in the United States, away from the palace, didn't mean he wouldn't treat Darcy like any other member of his staff.

Except Darcy had become more than an employee the second he'd plastered her up against the wall and kissed the hell out of her.

Last night their phone conversation had stimulated him in ways he hadn't expected. Sleep had been a long time coming and he had a feeling he'd be in the same predicament tonight. For the next several months, in fact, if they didn't end up just giving in to their desires.

He needed to get his head on straight and figure out how to tell Darcy about this trip. He actually loved the thought of taking her to his home country. He could only hope she'd take the news of his royal status well and agree to go with him. Colin had just started doing squats with the weight bar across his shoulders when his cell chimed from the bench behind him. Of all his exercises, this was the one that nearly killed his back and leg so he welcomed the distraction.

Dropping the bar back into place, he turned and smiled when he saw the name on the screen. He should've expected this.

"Is this going to be a ritual?" he asked in lieu of saying hello.

Darcy's soft laugh greeted him. "I just wanted to tell you again how much I appreciate the clothes. You didn't have to do anything like that for me, and saying thanks seems so inadequate, but...thanks."

Colin gripped the phone, wishing she'd come down and thank him in person. From her soft tone, he knew she was feeling a bit insecure, most likely about the money, which meant absolutely nothing to him. He had an exorbitant amount of it, so why shouldn't he be able to spend it on people he cared about?

"You're more than welcome," he replied, playing it safe instead of telling her what he really wanted to say. "But you don't have to keep thanking me."

"Maybe I just wanted to hear your voice."

Colin froze as she tossed back the words he'd given her last night. "You hear my voice all day."

"It's not the same with Iris around."

Closing his eyes, Colin reached out and rested his arm on the cool bar. He dropped his head and contemplated how to approach this shaky ground, because each step could set off a series of events he either didn't want or wasn't ready for. "You can come to the gym if you want to hear my voice," he said, hoping she'd take him up on his offer.

"No. This is best. I just…this is so silly."

"What were you going to say?"

Her pause had him lifting his head, listening for the slightest noise in the background. Was she already in bed? Had she lain there and thought of him?

"When I talked to you on the phone last night it was as if we were alone, just without the pressure of being alone." She laughed, then let out a groan. "Forget it. I'm not making sense."

She made perfect sense. Everything about her and this crazy situation made sense to him at this point in his chaotic life.

"Maybe we should pretend we're alone and we don't have to have any boundaries," he stated, his mouth spouting off words before he could fully filter his thoughts. "What if you were here with me now? Or what if I was up there with you? If we were just two people who met and there was nothing holding us back from taking what we wanted, what would you do?"

Silence greeted him and he knew without a doubt images were flooding Darcy's mind because they sure as hell were playing through his.

"What would you do if I showed up at your bedroom door right now?" he whispered.

He knew he was torturing himself. Unfortunately, he fantasized about Darcy whether he was speaking the words aloud or keeping the thoughts to himself.

"If nothing stood in our way, I'd let you in."

Colin wasn't sure whether to be thrilled or angry at this torturous piece of information. At least she came right out and said the words, but words meant nothing without action.

"What would we do after I came in?" he asked.

Her soft laugh enveloped him. "I'm not having phone sex with you."

"I wasn't headed there." Though now that she'd put that thought in his mind, he wouldn't object to a little phone sex. "Tell me, Darcy. Once

I came to your room and you let me in, what would happen?"

"Everything I've been dreaming about," she whispered. "But dreams aren't always meant to come true."

That sad tone of her voice said so much more than her actual words. He knew she'd been saving for an adoption. He wished he could be the man to give her what she wanted, but he was in no position to give anything unless it was financial or sexual. All superficial things, yes—anything involving his heart or too many emotions, hell no. He wasn't naive. He figured if things were different they may actually have a shot at something special, something more meaningful than intimacy. But how could they pursue anything beyond that when she had no idea who he was and he had no idea who he wanted to be?

A muffled sniff slid through the phone and Colin gripped the device tighter. "I'm coming up."

"No. Colin, you can't." Another sniff. "This is good, just talking. I haven't really talked about my feelings for a long time."

"You're crying."

He hated the thought of her lying up there upset, most likely over a bad memory that had been triggered by what he'd said. Colin wanted her happy, wanted that light in her eyes he'd become familiar with and he wanted to break down every damn wall she'd erected between them.

"I'm fine," she assured him. "It's getting late and I need to get up early for my workout."

"You have a standing invitation to work out with me."

"I know."

She still wouldn't take the offer, but he had to remind her anyway. He wanted to be here for her, to give his support, and that thought scared the hell out of him. Taking on someone else's problems was not going to help him solve his own and would only push him deeper into Darcy's life…a place he couldn't allow himself to be.

"Good night, Darcy."

"'Night, Colin."

He disconnected the call and resisted the urge to throw the phone across the room. This was a dangerous game he was playing with her. Not only were her feelings obviously involved, he had a sense her heart was teetering on the brink, too. That wasn't his ego talking, either. He didn't know if he had it in him to give her his heart. He knew he wanted her on a primal level and he was fully aware that his emotional connection with her was stronger than he'd intended, but there were so many uncertainties.

On the other hand, he wasn't too keen on the idea of another man capturing her heart, either, which left him in quite a predicament.

He had some decisions to make in his personal life here and back on Galini Isle. No matter what path he chose, Colin feared he'd be making a mistake and now there were even more lives—and hearts—on the line.

Colin kicked a ball to Iris, and just as she went to raise her leg the ball rolled right by her, causing her to laugh hysterically just like the past seventeen times he'd purposely kicked it by her.

Darcy swallowed the lump in her throat. A child's laughter was the sweetest noise, and by the looks of Colin's little game, he thought so, too..

The day was too beautiful for them to eat inside so Darcy had decided to set up lunch in the outside eating area. The father-daughter duo was having so much fun, they hadn't spotted her yet and Darcy was enjoying the view. Colin epitomized what fatherhood was all about. Spending time with his child, putting work on hold and not caring if he was getting texts or emails.

Exactly what Darcy would want for the father of her child if she could've had children. But she had to wonder what profession allowed him to have such flexibility. He'd mentioned that he managed a large group back home. Maybe he delegated most of his tasks. She could totally see him in a position of power and authority.

After pouring fresh iced tea into two glasses and placing a sippy cup of juice on the table, Darcy stood back and double-checked to make sure she hadn't forgotten anything. She was trying out a new recipe on Colin and she hoped he'd like it. Finding healthy dishes that weren't an all-day task to prepare was proving to be more difficult than she'd thought.

Smoothing her hands down her new mint-green shorts, Darcy headed out into the yard. Blades of grass tickled her bare feet as she crossed the lawn. Shielding her eyes from the afternoon sun with her hand, she continued to take in the beautiful image of the sexiest man she'd ever met playing with the sweetest little girl she'd ever cared for.

To look at them right now, one would never know a piece of their life had been ripped away when his wife passed. On a positive note, Iris wouldn't remember the pain of losing her mother. But she wouldn't have any mother-daughter memories to cherish. Darcy's mother hadn't died, but she had abandoned her at a young age. Still, Darcy's grandmother had always been there and was an amazing role model.

Colin glanced up, catching her gaze and pulling her from her thoughts. "You come out to play?" he asked.

"I set up lunch on the patio," she replied, rushing to play on Iris's side. Darcy kicked the ball back to Colin. "I figured we could eat out here today."

Iris clapped as Colin sent the ball back. "Deedee kick it."

For the next couple minutes, Darcy and Colin carried on a game. Before she knew it, the competition had turned serious and she was all over the yard, rounding him with the ball, dodging any attempt he tried to get back control. Colin thought he could outmaneuver her. Wasn't he in for a surprise? She was no stranger to kicking a ball around.

Finally, Darcy had mercy on him and she kicked the ball hard, sending it soaring through the air. Colin jumped, his arms extended above his head, and caught it with his hands.

"I'm raising the white flag," he panted.

Darcy resisted the urge to bend at the waist and draw in some much-needed air. She'd gotten in her second workout of the day, but she wasn't about to admit she was still out of shape and thrilled he'd called a halt to their impromptu game.

"How about we eat?" she suggested, reaching down to take Iris's hand. "I have fresh tea and I desperately need a drink."

Once they were all settled, Darcy sat next to Iris to help her with her food if necessary. Colin took a look at his plate and smiled.

"This looks great."

His verbal approval shouldn't have had her so excited. She'd only grilled some pineapple and chicken and put a homemade glaze over it. Nothing too fancy.

"Were you an athlete in school?"

Darcy sipped her glass of tea, welcoming the cold, refreshing drink. "I played soccer, actually. My school was big, so we had our own girls' team."

"You were pretty quick out there."

Darcy shrugged, even though a bit of pride burst through her at his statement. "Not as quick as I used to be. After graduating and helping Gram full time, I lost most of my stamina. As I've said before, I'm pretty out of shape now."

"I've already told you, your shape is just fine."

Darcy expected to look up and find him staring at her, but he was cutting into his chicken. Apparently the comment he kept throwing her way didn't affect him the way it did her. He tossed the words out so matter-of-factly, yet they meant so much to her. More than he could ever know.

"Your new clothes look nice on you."

Iris kicked her little feet in the highchair, causing the whole thing to wiggle, sending her sippy cup to the ground. Darcy retrieved it and set it back on the tray.

"For what you spent, they better," she joked.

Silence settled in for a bit before Iris started gibbering. Darcy didn't mind the quiet meal. There was no awkwardness surrounding them, only the peaceful, bright sunshine and the beauty of the lush backyard. It was times like this that Darcy could imagine slipping into the role of something so much more than a nanny.

"Did you play any sports in school?" she asked, trying to distract herself from her wayward thoughts.

Colin's fork froze halfway to his mouth, a naughty smile flirted around his lips. "I pretty much concentrated on girls and defying my father."

Darcy could easily see that. "What about your mother?"

"She was killed in an auto accident when I was younger."

Darcy's heart ached for him. He'd lost his mother and his wife? How much could a man take in one lifetime? So much heartache, yet he still smiled, still pushed forward and created a wonderful life for his own daughter.

"I shouldn't have asked," Darcy stated, slicing into her pineapple. "That was rude."

"You can ask me anything you want," he told her. "There's no need to be sorry. You didn't do anything wrong."

"No, but I don't want to bring up bad memories."

With a slight shrug, Colin reached for his tea. "The memories are always there. Not talking about them won't make them disappear."

Once Iris was finished, Darcy tidied her up and wiped off the tray. After taking a load of dishes into the kitchen, she came back out. Colin had pretty much cleaned up the rest and had his own stack of dishes in hand.

"I would've gotten those," she told him. "Just set them inside and I'll clean up later."

He didn't say a word as he passed. Darcy pulled Iris from her highchair and took her back out into the yard to continue the game of ball before the toddler went in for her nap.

Running in the grass, laughing and playing with a little one may have been something Darcy had dodged for years, but honestly this was exactly what she needed.

But the way they'd settled in almost like a family terrified Darcy because falling for a baby was one thing, but falling for the baby's father was another problem altogether. Yet the more time she spent with Colin, the more she saw what an amazing, giving man he was and the more she wanted him.

She was done denying herself.

Twelve

For the past week, Darcy had spoken to Colin on the phone every night before bed. There was something soothing about hearing that low, sultry voice without having to look him in the eyes or be distracted by that hard body. She loved their talks, which ranged from joking to flirting to borderline naughty.

They'd also had some serious moments. Moments that probably wouldn't have happened in the light of day or face-to-face. For some reason saying personal things on the phone was relaxing—almost therapeutic. She'd shared memories of her grandmother and he'd shared stories about how he and his brother used to rock climb together.

Darcy shifted against the sheets, the satin of her chemise sliding over her heated skin. Her gaze traveled to the phone on her nightstand. They'd already hung up for the night, but she needed more.

Before she lost her nerve, Darcy picked up her phone and called him back.

"Forget something?" he answered.

Oh, the replies she could throw back.

"I wasn't ready for bed." At least not alone. "Mind talking a bit more?"

"Not at all. You're a welcome distraction from this office work."

Darcy slid from bed and padded down the hall, careful not to speak when she passed Iris's door. For once she was going to be spontaneous, she was going to take what she wanted and live for the moment because there was no way she would walk out of here with regrets when her term ended.

There was only so much a woman could take.

"Something specific on your mind?"

Easing down the stairs, guided by only the

soft glow of the dimmed chandelier in the foyer, Darcy smiled. "Too many things to list."

Some shuffling and cursing in his native language had Darcy pausing, her hand on the banister at the base of the steps. "Everything okay?" she asked.

Colin laughed. "Yeah, just making a mess here."

Darcy knew that as soon as she hit the hallway he'd hear her talking, so she took a seat on the bottom step, curled her feet up onto the step below and looped her arms around her knees.

"If you wanted something more than anything in the world, but there were obstacles in your way, what would you do?"

"Are we going to pretend we aren't talking about you?" he asked.

"I'm pretending," she said with a smile, even though he couldn't see her. "You don't have to."

"Then pretend it's me," he told her. "When I want something, I find a way to claim it at any cost. I may not get it in the time frame I want, but eventually with enough patience, I make it mine."

Closing her eyes, Darcy let his strong words

push through that wall of fear she'd tried so hard to hide behind.

"What if time isn't on your side?" she whispered.

"What is it you want, Darcy?"

His question, nearly a whisper, too, told her he knew exactly what she wanted…or whom she wanted.

"I started to come to you." She gripped the phone tighter as if she could somehow pull strength from him. "I'm afraid."

Admitting that really humbled her because she didn't want to be seen as weak or vulnerable. Colin was neither of those things and she didn't figure he'd find a woman who was so indecisive and fearful attractive.

"You think I'm not?"

That voice was in full surround sound. Darcy jerked her head up to see Colin standing before her, phone still to his ear. The glow from the light illuminated him, making him seem even larger than life.

Darcy laid her phone beside her on the step. "You're not scared," she countered, unsure of what else to say at this point.

Crouching down with a slight wince, Colin placed his phone next to hers before laying his hands over the arm that was still wrapped around her knee. "Just because I'm scared doesn't mean I'll let the fear control my emotions. I want you, and the second you said you were coming to me I had to meet you halfway."

The man truly didn't let anything get in his way, not fear, not worry for the unknown...absolutely nothing.

"Maybe—"

He cut her off as he claimed her mouth beneath his. His hands instantly cupped the side of her face and tipped her head for better access. Colin's body eased forward and Darcy realized he'd placed his knees on the bottom step, so she spread her legs to accommodate him.

The moment her bare thighs slid against the side of his ribs, she groaned into his mouth. She'd never been this turned on, this ready for a man, and he'd only started kissing her. Granted, she'd only been with one man in her life, but there was absolutely no comparison between this passionate moment and anything she'd experienced before.

Breaking away, Colin peered down, stroked

her bottom lip with his thumb and held her gaze. "Never hold back with me. I want it all."

At that firm command, he took her lips again. Shivers coursed through her as Colin trailed his hands down her bare arms then slid them around her waist. With only the silk of her chemise providing a barrier, the warmth of his hands seared her skin. Arching into him, she wanted more and she wanted it now.

In one swift move, Colin picked her up and changed their positions so he sat on the step and she straddled his thighs.

His eyes roamed over her body. "You really do sleep in a black chemise."

Without comment, Darcy did what she'd wanted to do since day one. She leaned forward and trailed her tongue across that ink scrolling over his shoulder and down to his pec. The muscles clenched beneath her touch and a low growl erupted from Colin. His hands came around to cup her backside, jerking her closer against his arousal.

Darcy trembled, clutching his shoulders. An ache even fiercer than before spread through her. There was nothing outside this moment. Not her financial issues, not her infertility, not the mystery surrounding Colin, because if she were honest, that only added to his allure. They were both taking what they wanted.

Colin moved one hand around, splaying it over her upper thigh. His thumb teased just beneath the edge of the lacy trim on her panties, each stroke coming closer to the spot where she needed him the most.

Forgetting the torture of tasting his inked skin and chiseled muscles, Darcy dropped her head to his shoulder as he finally slid his thumb inside the material. Those slow strokes over her heated center were going to be the death of her. Darcy tipped her hips, silently demanding more. She'd denied herself this pleasure for so long, she simply couldn't take much more.

Her breath hitched as he eased inside her, her fingertips curled into his skin. He continued to torture her slowly, yet with so much control and power, Darcy was having a hard time getting her mind around the emotions tugging her in all different directions. But what if she wasn't enough for him? What if she disappointed him once they really got down to it?

She froze, not wanting this moment of blissful perfection to end, because it felt too good, too perfect. Too right.

"I told you not to hold back with me again," he growled in her ear. "Stop tensing up and let go."

With one hand still stroking her, he used the other to jerk down the top of her chemise. The strap snapped apart as his mouth settled over her breast. Darcy arched back, crying out as the full-on sexual encounter washed over her, sending her spiraling into the most intense climax of her entire life.

Before her tremors could cease, Colin was shifting beneath her and she realized he was working his shorts from side to side to get them down. Quickly she assisted him and found herself hovering right above a very naked, very aroused Colin. Then he slid his other hand between them and gave her chemise a tug, tearing apart the seam in the middle.

"I owe you another shopping trip," he muttered against her lips. "This time I'll be in the dressing room."

Oh, mercy. Shopping for lingerie with this

man would be…heaven. They'd never make it out alive.

"I have protection in my office and in my room."

Darcy held his gaze, her mind trying to process the words because she was still in a euphoric state.

"I've been anticipating this moment so I was prepared." He nipped her lips, shifted his hips so his erection nudged her. "You have about two seconds to decide where this will happen."

"Whichever one we get to fastest."

Colin came to his feet, causing Darcy to stand on her not-so-steady legs. She didn't have to worry, though, because Colin lifted her once more, not in the romantic scoop she'd always read about or seen in movies, but hooking her legs around his waist, forcing her to wrap her entire body around him. Oh, yeah. This was the experience she wanted. Nothing mushy here, but full-out want, need and the snapping of the control they'd both been barely holding onto.

He moved down the wide, darkened hall toward his office. Only a small bronze desk lamp cast any light on the room. Still, with her wrapped all around him, Colin jerked open a drawer and tossed a foil package onto the glossy surface of the desk. Darcy nipped at his shoulder, earlobe and jawline. With protection taken care of, she wanted him. Now.

When he sat her on top of his desk, he eased back, taking her face in his hands. "You're sure?"

Darcy nodded. The intensity of his gaze and the way he held his lips firm told her he may have more to say, but instead he tore open the wrapper and covered himself before pulling her to the edge of the desk.

Darcy leaned back on her elbows, staring up at him and watching as he gazed back down at her. Colin's hands gripped her hips as he slid into her. When he caught her gaze, a tick visible in his jaw, she smiled. "Don't worry about going slow."

Something must have snapped because the next thing she knew he wasn't holding back…in any way.

Darcy's head fell back as pleasure engulfed her, as Colin claimed her. She'd never experienced anything so perfect, so all-consuming in her entire life.

Their frantic pace sent something from the desk

crashing to the floor, but she didn't care and the commotion didn't slow Colin down, either. She barely noticed papers shifting beneath her. With the way Colin's eyes were locked on hers, the way he held her waist with his strong hands and took her as if he owned her, Darcy didn't think she'd ever care about anything else again. He was completely ruining her for any other man.

Another wave crested over her and Darcy cried out, her legs tightening around Colin's waist. He jerked once more and stilled, his fingertips bruising her sides.

After they stopped trembling, Colin leaned over, his forehead resting against her shoulder.

"I haven't done that since before my accident," he muttered. "I was afraid I'd hurt you if I carried you and fell, but I had to try. I wanted you in my arms. I want to be the man you need."

He was that man and so much more. Darcy had wondered if her heart would get swept away with Colin because of his single-father status, but what she felt for him had nothing to do with his child, his finances or anything other than the fact that he alone turned her inside out and made her feel things she'd only ever fantasized about. He made her come alive in ways she never had before.

"If you give me a few minutes, I'll take you up to my room." His lips cruised over her damp skin, causing her to already want him again. "I need you in my bed."

Darcy didn't say a word. She would follow him to his bed. She'd follow him anywhere he asked.

Darcy's hair tickled the side of his face, but there was no way he was moving. She fit perfectly against his side, tucked snugly into him, as if she was made to be there. But right now, after taking her on his desk, and pleasuring her again once they'd arrived in his room, Colin didn't want to think any deeper than this blissful, sated feeling. He couldn't, wouldn't dive into that black hole of thoughts where all of his worries and fears about committing to another woman lived.

For the first time in months, he let loose and enjoyed his time with a refreshing woman who pulled him back to basic life…exactly what he'd been searching for.

With Darcy's arm across his abdomen and her leg across his thigh, the woman was staking her own claim and he had to admit, he liked it. He liked her. To know she wasn't into one-night stands completely humbled him. She'd been brave to initiate the encounter.

"I have a trip I need to take in a few days." His words cut through the darkened silence. "I'd like you to accompany me."

Sliding her fingertips up and down his abs, she asked, "Where are we going?"

"I need to go back home for an event," he told her, unable to reveal the rest of the details. "We will only be gone a few days."

Darcy shifted, easing up on one elbow to look down at him. His eyes had adjusted to the dark, plus the soft glow from the security monitors offered a dim light.

"Do I need to pack anything in particular?" she asked with a smile. "I've never been out of the country before."

She'd need a passport if she didn't have one and that could be problematic unless his assistant pulled some strings. They'd be flying in the palace jet, but still there was customs. He'd have his staff figure out the details.

"That blue dress would be a nice start," he told her. "But just be yourself. That's all you need to do."

She didn't have to go, she could stay behind, but he wanted her there. Granted he had a whole host of people who could care for Iris—maids, butlers, assistants, his sister-in-law. The list truly was endless.

But he wanted Darcy on his turf, he wanted to see how she fit into his life.

Colin nearly gasped as a realization dawned on him. He was falling for this woman in his arms. He was falling so hard, so fast, but he couldn't admit it fully, because what if she rejected him?

"You mentioned your parents had passed. Do you have siblings other than the brother you've mentioned?"

Her question pulled him from his thoughts.

Being here with Darcy, going into public without guards or paparazzi snapping photos was so different, so refreshing and so damn freeing. But he still felt as if he was letting down not only his country but Stefan. His brother was all Colin had left and putting the entire future of Galini Isle on Stefan's shoulders wasn't fair.

"Just Stefan and his wife Victoria."

"And they live in Greece?"

"Yes," he replied, fully enjoying the way her fingers continued to travel over his exposed torso. "What about you? No siblings, I assume."

"No. It was just my Gram and me after my parents split town. Apparently they weren't into the whole parenting thing and my Gram wasn't about to let me go into the foster system. I lived with her, worked with her and learned everything I know from the most amazing woman in the world."

No wonder Darcy was such a fighter. She'd had one person to depend on her entire life…a life spent caring for others. Colin had a whole army of people he depended on back home and he was running from them.

"Did you once mention wanting to adopt a baby of your own?" he asked.

A soft sigh escaped her, tickling his shoulder. "I would love to adopt, but it's expensive and my business needs to get back on track again. I'm afraid by the time I get all settled financially and go through the process, I'll be too old."

"You're young enough."

Her fingertips traced his tattoo the same way her tongue had earlier. She'd damn near had his eyes rolling back in his head.

"I know, but given the experience I had with my ex…it just hurts." She settled her head back in the crook of his arm, but continued to run her hand over his chest and abs as if she couldn't get enough…which suited him just fine. "To know you share your dreams, open your heart to someone and have them lie and betray you like that. I'm not sure I'll ever get over that pain. My dreams were put on hold and I'm not sure I'll ever get them back."

Colin swallowed. He wasn't the same as this ex, so he shouldn't feel guilty about lying.

Still, he wanted to clear the air about something.

"The last woman I was with was my wife," he told her, hating this topic in bed, but needing to get it out. "I know I mentioned that before, but I wanted you to know I may have been reckless as a teen and into my early twenties, but between marrying, the accident and then Iris, I've calmed down. I didn't want you to think I was using you because you were here and convenient."

"I know you're not," she murmured. "I've only been with one man before you. I just don't take the time to date and a fling is not something I can do."

Colin laughed, earning him a smack. "Sorry," he chuckled.

"You know what I mean," she defended. "I'm going to be here several months, so I hope tonight wasn't a one-time thing. I mean, I guess that should've been discussed, but I assumed—"

Colin rolled over, pinning her beneath him and cutting off her words.

"I plan on having you as often as you'll allow me to," he told her. As he looked into her bright eyes, he knew he had to tell her the rest. "I need to tell you why we're going back home."

She stared up at him, her eyes locking directly onto his. "Let's not talk right now." She spread her legs so he could settle firmly between them. "I only want to think about right now, with you, in your bed."

The trip could wait.

Colin smoothed her hair away from her face, nipped at her lips. "Maybe I want you to just lay back, think of absolutely nothing but how good everything feels."

He didn't wait for her reply as he started kissing his way down her body. When Darcy clutched the sheets, he smiled as he continued his path.

The next few months were going to be amazing.

Thirteen

Darcy wore only Colin's T-shirt as she maneuvered around the kitchen getting breakfast ready. She'd skipped her early morning workout and opted to stay snuggled next to Colin's warm, strong body. Of course she'd gotten enough of a calorie burn last night, in the middle of the night and again this morning.

Not only had he ruined her for any other man, he'd ruined her for any other workout. Why exercise with some cold piece of machinery when she could get a thorough workout with a hunky man ready to meet her every need?

Iris sat in her high chair, tapping her spoon

against the tray and babbling. Every now and then a coherent word would slip out, but she was mostly just entertaining herself while Darcy cooked up some pancakes.

Colin had wanted to shower early, so he should be joining them soon. Everything about the morning after wasn't at all uncomfortable the way she'd heard people say. If anything it was very…domestic and normal.

The chime at the gate jerked Darcy from stirring the pancake batter. Who on earth was trying to visit this early in the morning? As long as no one on the inside of the house buzzed the guest in, they wouldn't get beyond the gate, unless they had the code. Darcy wasn't allowing anyone to pass through because Colin hadn't mentioned he was expecting a guest and this wasn't her house.

A moment later Colin came down the steps wearing a pair of running shorts and nothing else but a tan and the tat. She'd explored that body, tasted and touched it, yet the sight of him still had her knees weakening. How had her life gone from being so bleak, so depressing, to something that sparked hope and new life?

"Was that the gate alarm?" he asked as he bent down to give Iris a kiss and ruffle her curly bedhead.

"Yeah. I didn't answer the call because I didn't know if you were expecting anybody or not."

Darcy went back to mixing, wondering how she should act this morning. The entire scene seemed so family-like, so perfect, and she feared she'd make a mistake and this dream would be over.

"I'm not. Wonder who wanted in this early in the morning?" he mumbled. "I take it you weren't expecting anyone."

Darcy laughed as she poured the batter for several pancakes onto the warm griddle. "Do you honestly think I've invited friends to come over?"

"You can, you know."

She glanced his way and rolled her eyes. "I may take you up on that. I've texted my friends, but I've just been too busy to entertain."

"You can entertain me anytime." He crossed the spacious kitchen, rounded the island and slid a hand up beneath the T-shirt she wore. "You look better in this shirt than I ever did."

How could she not get swept into the fantasy this whole scene represented? She had to keep everything separate—her attraction for Colin in one part of her heart, her love for Iris in another. And there was no room for this family bonding. Colin and Iris weren't her family no matter how much she wished they were. Being swept into a love affair was already uncharted territory, but allowing her heart to get caught up in this fantasy was only going to crush her in the end when she walked away alone.

The doorbell chimed, causing Darcy and Colin to freeze. His hand slid out of the shirt, leaving her cold where his warmth had been.

"Stay here. There's only one person who has this code besides us."

Colin didn't look happy. Who would have the code? They'd been here for two months and nobody had used it yet, so why now?

As soon as the front door opened, another male voice filled the home. She pulled the pancakes off the griddle and set them aside on a spare plate. After flicking the griddle off, Darcy cut up a half of a pancake for Iris. Raised voices from the foyer had Darcy plucking Iris from her highchair.

Who was here? Should she try to go out the back and get to a neighbor for help? Darcy cursed herself for only wearing a T-shirt. She scooted closer to the side of the kitchen that was closest to the foyer to see if she could hear better but not be seen since she was hardly dressed for company.

"Are you going to let me in?" an unfamiliar male voice asked. Whoever this man was, he had the same sexy accent as Colin.

Colin spoke vehemently, again in Greek— what sounded like a curse. Moments later the door closed. Whoever was here, Colin knew him but he was a stranger to Darcy. Great. Her attire screamed that she'd just gotten out of bed...her lover's bed.

"Nice place," the other man commented. "But are you ready to come back and forget this notion of living in the States?"

"You should've called," Colin replied, his tone implying the guest still wouldn't have been welcome.

"We've talked nearly every single day. I wanted to surprise you."

Footsteps echoed, growing louder. Darcy moved toward the island and put Iris back into her high chair. She'd just taken her seat when a man who could be Colin's twin stepped into the room, Colin right on his heels.

"Stefan, this is Darcy."

She hadn't been able to hide behind the island in time and the man's eyes traveled over her, taking in her oversized T-shirt, the hem of the boxers peeking out from beneath it and her bare legs before going to Iris and then back to Colin.

"I'm sorry," he said, turning back toward Colin. "I didn't know…wait, is this your nanny?"

Darcy cringed and turned to concentrate on cutting up Iris's food. Whatever was going on with these two, she wanted no part of it. Clearly they had issues that didn't involve her. Well, maybe they did now.

"Stefan," Colin growled. "Not a word."

"I'm just trying to figure things out." Stefan shook his head and propped his hands on his hips. "Are you giving up your title, turning your back on your country and the throne for someone you barely know?"

Darcy froze. *Title? Throne?*

Slowly, she lifted her gaze to Colin. He stared back at her as if he was waiting to see her reaction, too.

"Shut the hell up, Stefan," Colin nearly shouted. "Apologize to Darcy. She has nothing to do with my decision and you know I'm taking the full six months to think this through."

"My apologies," Stefan said, turning and tipping his head toward Darcy. The worried look etched across his face told Darcy he was sincere. "I mean no disrespect to you. I was just taken aback. I've been waiting for my brother to come home, and I knew he'd found a reason to stay for now. I certainly didn't mean to take my shocked state out on you. Actually, Mikos has told me quite a bit about you and I want to thank you for being so kind to my niece."

"There's nothing to worry about with me," Colin cut in before Darcy could respond. "I'm still unclear on my decision."

"Mikos." The other man stepped closer to Colin. "Are you seriously that happy here that you're still confused? Have you not missed anything about Galini Isle or the people who love you?"

Darcy swallowed, terrified to ask, but needing to know. "Why is he calling you Mikos and what does he mean by throne and title?"

Colin's eyes closed on a sigh, but before he could answer, the other man turned to face her completely. "I'm calling him Mikos because that's his name and he's a prince from Galini Isle, a small country off the coast of Greece."

Darcy had no idea what to say, what to do. All those times they'd talked, every single day they'd shared together over the last two months and he couldn't find it in his heart to tell her any of that? Not even his real name?

Tears blurred her vision, but even through the hurt and confusion, she had a baby to care for. That was what he was paying her for, right?

Whatever game he was playing by seducing her, it was clear that she was pretty much just hired help. Had he ever seen her as anything more or had he been laughing at her this entire time?

"Darcy—"

With a jerk of her head and a glare, Darcy cut off whatever Colin, Mikos…whoever, had been about to say.

"You haven't told her?" the other man asked. "Classy, Mikos. Real classy."

* * *

Colin was seriously fighting the urge to punch his brother in the face. First of all, to show up unannounced was rude even for Stefan. Second, how the hell did he fix this with Darcy now? The last thing he wanted was for her to be hurt, for her to feel as though she'd been betrayed again.

But he'd lied because been so dead set on keeping his identities separate. He'd gotten so wrapped up in her, in this life, that he hadn't given much thought to consequences. He'd been thinking only of himself. Just as he had with Karina, and look how that had turned out.

"Let me feed her," Colin offered, stepping forward. "You go change."

Her hands shook with each bite she put in Iris's mouth, but Darcy didn't even turn to answer him.

"Darcy." Stefan also stepped forward. "I apologize for coming in like this and dropping a bomb on you. I'd assumed my brother would've told you about his status. Why don't you go change and I'll feed my niece? I haven't seen her for a long time."

Now Darcy lifted her head, gave a slight nod and headed out of the room, careful to go around the island to avoid getting too close Stefan and Colin. She didn't say a word, didn't look either of them in the eye.

Her pain lingered after she was gone. Colin would never forget the angst that had washed over her face right before she slid up that invisible wall and avoided looking at him. Good God, what had he done?

"I could kill you for that," Colin muttered.

Stefan leaned his hip against the island and forked up another bite for Iris. He made an airplane motion and some ridiculous noise to get her to open for him. Of course she clapped and kicked her feet, oblivious to the turmoil going on.

"Don't be angry with me that you kept the truth hidden. If you like the woman, and I have to assume you do because you're still here, then she deserved the truth."

Colin slammed his fist onto the counter. "You have no idea what has happened so don't even think about assuming you do." But Stefan was absolutely right. Why hadn't he seen this coming?

"It's about time you're showing emotion for someone else." A smile spread across Stefan's face. "I'm glad to see you're living again. Are you and Darcy serious?"

Colin rolled his eyes. This wasn't up for debate. He went to get a plate, but suddenly he wasn't hungry anymore. Right now Darcy was upstairs, most likely angry, hurt, maybe even crying, because he thought he could keep all the balls in the air and have control over every facet of his life.

"I don't know what we are," Colin defended himself. He thought he knew what he wanted, but would Darcy ever speak to him again? Did his wants even matter at this point?

Stefan paused, bite in midair. "She's wearing your shirt and whisker burn, cooking your breakfast and caring for your child. I'd say that's pretty serious. Yet you still lied to her. It makes me wonder why."

"I'm paying her to care for Iris."

Stefan glanced around the island, found a sippy cup and passed it to Iris before turning his focus back to Colin. "And the rest? I know you're not paying her for that, and this is the first woman you've shown interest in since Karina."

"I don't give a damn what you think right now.

I was planning on coming home for the ball, you didn't have to show up unannounced."

Stefan shrugged. "Last time we spoke you told me you weren't sure if you were coming back. I merely came to talk some sense into you. Victoria had to stay behind to get last minute things prepared for the event or she would've been right here with me."

Colin raked a hand over his still damp hair. "Watch Iris for me. I need to go upstairs and talk to Darcy. Stay down here and shut the hell up next time you see her. You've done enough damage."

Colin didn't wait for Stefan to confirm anything, he just turned and stormed from the room. His back was killing him, as was his leg after all the extra activities he'd participated in last night, but he was determined to march right into Darcy's room and set things straight.

He had nothing planned to say, had no clue what state he'd find her in or what was even going through her mind. He was about to enter unstable territory and it terrified him because he realized that what she thought was important.

Not only did he not want to be the one to hurt

her, but he also wanted to be the one she counted on. So many people had turned away from her, betrayed her in one form or another.

And he'd just added his name to the list. Surely he could make this up to her somehow.

Yet he stood outside her bedroom door, staring at the barrier as if the inanimate object could offer insight. What a mess he'd made, all because he'd been too self-absorbed, too wrapped up in Darcy and his hormones to truly see the big picture. Not that he saw any clearer now, but he did know one thing, he still wanted Darcy and he'd make damn sure he would fix this disaster he'd caused.

Colin tapped his knuckles on the door. It hadn't latched completely so the weight of his hand eased it open just enough for him to see her standing across the room, her back to him, as she looked out onto the backyard.

"I know you want to be alone," he started, staying in her doorway. "But we need to talk."

Darcy's shoulders stiffened, the only sign she'd even heard him. Silence settled heavily between them, when only an hour ago they were lying side by side in his bed. At least she'd thrown on some pants so he didn't have to be tortured further by the sight of her bare legs. He could still feel them wrapped around him, entwined with his.

"I didn't set out to lie to you, even though that's how it looks." He had to keep talking. If she wasn't ordering him out, then he knew she was listening. "I have a lot going on back home, so much that I didn't want to talk about it with anyone. I wanted to separate myself from that part of my life for a while to get my head on straight. I had to put Iris's needs first and keeping our identity a secret was one of my top priorities."

He paused, giving her a chance to speak if she wanted. When she remained silent, he pushed on.

"I wish I could blame my brother for barging in here and dropping that bomb like that, but it's my fault you didn't know." Taking a risk, Colin stepped further into the room, raking a hand down his face as he carefully chose the right words. "You matter to me, Darcy. More than I want to admit and more than I thought someone could after Karina. I don't want this to come between us."

Darcy whirled around. The tear tracks on her cheeks crippling him in ways words never could.

"You mean you don't want your lies to keep me out of your bed?" she threw back. "Because isn't that all we have between us? Our arrangement was never meant to be more than temporary. So, for once since I've known you, be honest."

Colin swallowed the fear, the anger. He'd brought it all upon himself. He had to stand here and take it like a man. He deserved every word, every bit of rage she wanted to fling at him.

"You're only up here because you want to continue what we started last night." Darcy shook her head and laughed, swiping at her damp face. "I was such a fool. You were probably laughing at me the entire—"

She gasped, her eyes darting to her closet before her face crumbled. Turning away, she let out a low moan as she hugged her arms around her midsection.

"You knew I had nothing and there you were, throwing your money around," she whispered.

Colin started to cross to her because he couldn't stand the anguish lacing her voice, but she spun to face him, holding him with her hurt-filled stare. He stopped only a few feet from her.

"Did you get a kick out of giving to the needy?"

she asked, her tone nothing but mocking. "Did you enjoy knowing you had everything, while I had absolutely nothing? Money, power, control. You literally played me, never once thinking how this would affect me."

"I never played you," he corrected. "I wouldn't have told anyone I employed here about my life on Galini Isle. And I damn well did worry about you. Every single day we grew closer I worried how this would affect you, but I didn't know what to say or how to even approach it."

Her eyes narrowed. "Because you're a coward. Apparently running from the truth is what you do. You fled your home when you obviously didn't want to face responsibilities there."

How could she ever understand that he hadn't been strong enough to face his royal duties as a widowed father, trying to bring up a duchess? How could she ever grasp how much was involved in being a prince raising a child in the kingdom? What if Iris didn't want the title that came along with her prestigious family name?

At some point this getaway had turned from him finding himself to him deciding what was going to be best for the future of his daughter.

"I have to go back in a couple days," he told her, forcing himself to put up a strong front because the sight of her so broken was damn near crippling. "I still want you to come with me."

Pain-filled laughter erupted from Darcy. "You're insane. I'm not going anywhere with you. This isn't some fairy tale, Colin or Mikos or whatever the hell you want to be called. This is my life and I'm not just running to some island in Greece because you snap your fingers and expect me to."

"I want you to go to be with Iris," he explained, hoping she'd cave because he didn't realize how much he needed her to be there on his turf until this moment. "She's used to you, she's comfortable with you and I'd rather have you caring for her than any of my assistants."

Throwing her arms in the air, Darcy pivoted and moved around him to stand on the other side of the room. "You're something else. You probably have multiple people at your disposal, yet you continue to want to torture me. Why? Are you enjoying this power trip?"

Clenching his fists at his sides, he watched as

she began to pace. "I'm not enjoying any part of this."

"You're using Iris as a bargaining tool." She stopped and propped her hands on her hips. "You're using her to get me to come with you."

"I'm being honest," he told her. "You wanted honesty, I'm laying it out there. I tried to tell you this morning. I know that's a convenient thing to say considering the timing, but it's the truth. I want you to see my country. I want you to be the one to care for Iris while I'm home because I will be facing many challenges there."

He didn't want to get too far into everything that he was running away from. Darcy wasn't in the right frame of mind to hear it and he wasn't ready to admit how weak and vulnerable he truly was.

Darcy pursed her lips together, then nodded. "Fine, but if you want to throw that money around so much, then I want double my original pay for the entire six months. If I'm traveling, then I deserve to be compensated accordingly."

This was probably not the time to say he was proud of her for standing up for herself, for playing hardball and fighting for what she wanted.

Most women would've packed their bags and left. He'd always known she was a fighter and she was coming back at him full force.

She was the only woman who'd ever challenged him. What would he do on Galini Isle without her by his side? He wasn't about to find out.

"Done," he said without second thought. "On one condition."

She quirked a brow. "What?"

"When we're at the palace, you have to do what I say. No questions."

"I don't think—"

"Do you want the money?"

Darcy stilled, and her nostrils flared as her cheeks reddened. "You're despicable."

No, he was desperate, but he'd never admit that aloud. "We'll leave Sunday evening and sleep on my jet."

"Of course you have a jet," she muttered before moving toward her door. "We're done here. I'll take care of Iris, I'll do everything a hired nanny does and she will be my number one priority. That doesn't include sleeping with my boss. From now on our relationship is strictly professional."

Crossing the room, Colin kept his gaze locked

onto hers. As he neared, her eyes widened but she never looked away. He stopped only a breath from her, then leaned down to whisper in her ear.

"I never set out to lie to you, Darcy. You have to believe me."

As he spoke, his lips caressed the side of her cheek. Just as she shivered, Colin eased back. Her hand came up to slap him, but he quickly gripped her wrist in midair.

"You're angry. Don't do something you'll regret later." Although he knew he deserved it.

Her eyes flared, filling with unshed tears. "I hate you."

He yanked her forward to fall against his chest. With one hand still holding onto her wrist, Colin hooked an arm around her waist. "There's a fine line between hate and passion," he said with a confidence he didn't quite feel.

Unable to resist temptation, Colin captured her lips, but let the brief kiss end for fear she'd bite him. He smiled down at her.

"Make sure to pack the blue dress for our trip."

He'd barely made it out her door before it slammed at his back.

Damn it. He had to do something. Somehow he

had to make this up to her. Losing Darcy was not an option, but he'd messed up. He didn't deserve her forgiveness, but that wouldn't stop him from doing everything in his power to earn it.

Fourteen

Darcy could dwell on the fact that her parents had abandoned her at a young age. She could also hone in the fact that the man she'd thought she loved had stolen every last penny she had to her name. She could even focus on her most recent betrayal: Colin keeping the colossal truth that he was a freaking prince from her. But Darcy opted to go a different route.

From now on, she would choose anger, because if she even attempted to shut it out, all she'd have left to face would be soul-crushing hurt. There was no time for that because there was an innocent child in all of this…a child Darcy had been hired to care for.

As much as Darcy wanted to take the initial half of her pay and leave Colin, she wouldn't abandon Iris. Darcy couldn't walk away, not when she knew all too well the feeling of rejection. But what would Colin do at the end of the six months? Did he have other arrangements set up or was he going back home? Did he even know himself?

Darcy continued to stare out the window of the car that had been waiting for them when they'd arrived at the private airstrip on Galini Isle. Iris had been sitting, securely strapped in, between her and Colin, and since they'd left LA Darcy had barely spoken a word to him unless it involved the baby. Nothing else needed to be said at this point, the damage was done.

Iris continued to sleep, which was a blessing because the poor thing had cried a good bit of the flight. Most likely the pressure in her ears had been getting to her. Even though exhaustion threatened to consume Darcy, too, she was too angry to be tired.

Beyond the obvious anger toward Colin, she was furious with herself because of her reaction to his parting shot in her room about still wanting her. He'd known just what to say, exactly the right way to deliver the words for the most impact.

Colin may have been a different man when he was with her, a man he'd made up, yet she still wanted him. Nobody had ever made her feel more beautiful, more wanted than he did. He'd wrapped his arms around her and kissed her as if he had every right in the world.

But that was all part of his game. He'd created a new life in America and she was just another prop. More than anything she wished she could switch her emotions off to avoid the hurt, but she simply wasn't wired that way.

The chauffeur pulled into a drive. Darcy noted the gate, guards and white columns as the car made its way onto the estate grounds. What was she doing here? She was going to spend the next few days in a palace. *A palace.* Only a few months ago she'd had to sleep in her car because she'd lost her condo, and now she was going to be staying in a freaking mansion in another country. She'd never even set foot outside of California before.

When they came to a stop, Darcy started to open her door, but Colin leaned a hand across where Iris slept and laid his other hand over Darcy's arm.

"They'll get your door," he told her.

Rolling her eyes, Darcy jerked from his grasp and opened her own damn door. Once she stepped out, she turned and reached in to gently unfasten and pull Iris from her seat. She slept on as Darcy cradled her against her shoulder.

"Ma'am." The driver held her door, tipping his head toward her. "I'll make sure your bags are brought in."

She nearly laughed. Her bag, singular, was still her ratty old suitcase that didn't suit palace living at all. Of course the clothes inside certainly did, considering they were purchased with royal money.

Ignoring Colin's attempt to put his hand on her and guide her, she stepped to the side and shot him a glare. "Just have someone show me where the nursery is and I'll take her in."

"I'll show you."

His tone left no room for argument. Whatever. She wasn't going to fight, not with sweet Iris in her arms. Darcy truly wanted the best for Iris, even if her father was a lying jerk.

The three-story mansion stretched along the grounds farther than any "home" Darcy had ever seen. Lush plants and vibrant flowers surrounded the palace, edged along the circular drive and flanked the steps leading up to the entrance. Guards in full military-looking uniforms stood at attention on either side of the door.

This world was definitely not hers. Everything about her life had been transformed the moment she'd met Colin. From the new clothes, her emotional state, her sexual experiences...every single aspect of her personal and professional life would never be the same.

Passing by guards, entering a grand home with a tiered fountain inside the entryway—*inside* the entryway—was stunning. Darcy shook her head as she followed Colin closely. As they passed random people...maids, men in suits, servants? Darcy noted that Colin would nod in greeting while the others would slightly bow. People actually bowed to the man.

Yes, they were worlds apart in every sense of the term because Darcy was on the same level as these people bowing to the man she wanted to throttle.

Colin led her toward a grand staircase that would make the iconic home from *Gone with the Wind* seem miniscule.

Colin turned before ascending the steps. "Why don't you let me carry her up?"

"I've got her and your back has been bothering you."

The corner of his mouth tipped as if he were holding back a smile. "You know me so well. And you care."

Darcy moved around him, refusing to even look at that handsome, sexy grin, those mocking, alluring blue eyes. "I saw you cringe when you stepped off the plane and again getting out of the car. And I only care about Iris."

As she started up, she knew he was behind her, most likely eyeing her rear end. That was fine, she couldn't stop him from looking, but she could prevent him from touching.

She had to prevent him from touching because if the man even tried to come on to her, she'd have a hard time holding it together. She couldn't ignore her emotions or hormones, no matter how much she wished her body would stop betraying her.

Once she reached the second floor, she turned back to see Colin gripping the banister, taking the steps more slowly than she'd thought he would. An unwelcome tug on her heart revealed the anger still rolling through her.

With one arm securing the sleeping baby, Darcy eased down a step and reached out her free hand. Colin froze, glancing from her hand to her face. She thought for sure his stubborn pride would have him swatting her away, but he put his hand in hers and squeezed. He climbed the last few steps with her support, without comment.

Once he righted himself, he moved down the hallway and Darcy was relieved they weren't heading up to the next floor because she highly doubted Colin could make it. Being on the plane for so long had most likely agitated his injury. His limp was a bit more prominent as he moved down the wide hallway. She wanted to reach for him again, but…she couldn't. Focusing on following him, she took in the luxurious surroundings.

Gold sconces adorned each section of wall between each door. The ceiling had scrolling artwork that she would have to admire later because

Colin had neared the end of the hall and was going into a bedroom.

Bedroom was seriously too loose a term. The area she entered was a condo all its own with a formal sitting area, open bedroom tucked away in the far corner and two sets of French doors that opened onto a balcony offering a breathtaking view of the ocean.

"This is the nursery?"

"This is your room. I've asked for Iris's stuff to be put in here so you can stay close to her and you won't have to be near me or anyone else."

The crib was nestled in the opposite corner along the same wall as the king-sized bed. Moving across the wide room, Darcy gently laid Iris in the crib, surprised when the little one nestled deeper into the mattress and let out a soft sigh.

Once Darcy was sure Iris was going to stay asleep, she turned and moved back to where Colin remained standing. His eyes were fixed on hers and, try as she might, she couldn't look away. She both hated this man and found herself drawn to him for unexplainable reasons.

"We'll be fine now." She hoped he'd take the

hint and leave. "I'm assuming someone will bring our things to this room."

Colin stepped closer to her, closing the gap between them. Darcy had to tip her head back to look up and hold his gaze.

"The formal ball is tomorrow night," he told her. "I want you there. With me."

This fairy tale was really starting to get out of control. She only wanted to be here with Iris. Getting dressed up and playing any other role wouldn't be a smart move.

"I'm your child's nanny," she informed him, forcing herself to ignore the thread of arousal winding though her at his intense stare. "I'm not your date for hire or one of your assistants you can order around. Everything changed when you opted to keep the truth from me."

A smile spread across his face, showcasing that dimple she'd once found sexy.... His palms slid up her bare arms, curved over her shoulders and glided on up to frame her face.

"You forget you agreed to do what I want while we're here."

The reminder was the equivalent of cold water being thrown in her face.

"You can't use me like this," she whispered.

"I'm not using you," he replied, his face now hovering just above hers. "I'm simply taking what I want and I want you on my arm during the ball."

Another layer of anger slid through her. "Is that why you told me to pack the blue dress?"

"No. I don't want anyone else to see you in that dress." His thumb stroked her bottom lips, his gaze honed in on her mouth. "That dress is for my eyes only. You'll wear it for dinner tonight."

"I don't want dinner with you," she threw back, though her voice wasn't as strong as she'd hoped it would be. "You said I didn't have to leave my room if I didn't want to."

That thumb kept sliding back and forth with just enough pressure to have Darcy nearly begging him to kiss her. Darn hormones betraying her common sense.

"You're not leaving your room," he stated. "Dinner will be delivered."

He stepped away, leaving her aching, wanting more and all he'd done was use that low, sultry voice and fondled her lips. How pathetic could she be?

"Be ready by seven."

With that he turned and walked out of the room. Darcy continued to stare at the door long after he'd left. How dare that man expect her to just be at his beck and call? If he wanted to have dinner with her, fine, but she had a surprise of her own for him and it sure as hell didn't involve that sexy blue dress.

Darcy was playing hide-and-seek with Iris— which was quite easy in a room of this size with the adjoining bath and colossal walk-in closet— when someone knocked on her door.

Iris squealed and ran to the door, standing on her tiptoes to try to reach the knob. Darcy laughed and eased Iris back so she could open the door.

Darcy was greeted by one of the most beautiful women she'd ever seen in her life. The stranger was holding a long, white garment bag.

"Hi, Darcy," the woman said with a wide, radiant smile. "I'm Victoria Alexander. I'm Stefan's wife. Would you mind if I came in for just a moment?"

Iris sneaked around Darcy and started reaching for Victoria.

"Hi, sweetheart." Victoria bent slightly, shifting the bag to the side so she could give Iris a kiss on her head. "How's my big girl? I missed you so much."

Darcy stepped aside and let Victoria pass through. Victoria crossed the room and hung the garment bag over the door leading into the closet area.

When she turned back around, she scooped Iris into her arms and squeezed her. The instant burn to Darcy's eyes was unexpected. Iris obviously had so many people who loved her, who needed her. Darcy had to face the harsh reality that she was just a random employee of the prince passing through. The impact on Darcy was huge, life-altering, but Iris would never even remember her.

"First of all, let me tell you how sorry I am about this whole thing." Iris wiggled in Victoria's arms until she was let free. "Stefan explained everything to me and I am embarrassed that he dropped what I'm sure was shocking news when he visited. I'm even more embarrassed that my brother-in-law took it upon himself to lie to you by omission. The Alexander men can be infuriating and you were dealt a double dose."

Darcy clasped her hands in front of her, not quite sure how to take this woman, but from the looks of things, she could be an ally.

"I'm from LA, too, so I know this whole royalty thing can be overwhelming at times," Victoria went on, offering a sweet smile. "I just want you to know that while you're here, please feel free to let me know if you need anything. Stefan and Mikos can be quite…difficult to communicate with at times. They seem to have their minds set on certain agendas and tend to let nothing stand in their way."

Darcy laughed. "That's one way of putting it."

"Mikos really is an amazing man." Victoria's eyes darted to where Iris was running around the spacious room, dodging the chaise longue, weaving through the sheers by the patio doors. "He's a wonderful father and he's been through so much. Don't be so quick to judge him when he's clearly made a drastic mistake."

Darcy shook her head and sighed. "I'm just the nanny. It's not my place to judge."

"If you were just the nanny, I wouldn't have

spent the last two days making a dress for you to wear at the ball tomorrow." Victoria pointed to the garment bag. "Once you try it on, let me know if it needs to be altered. Mikos was pretty specific in his instructions."

Darcy stared at Victoria, then to the bag. "What? You made a dress?"

"I'm a designer. It's what I do." Victoria shrugged. "Sounds silly, I know, considering I'm also the queen, but that's just a title. I was designing dresses before I ever married into the Alexander family and I didn't want to lose my identity."

A bit taken aback, Darcy made her way to the garment bag and slid the zipper down. Peeling away the protective plastic, she gasped at the shimmering, pale blue formal gown. With one shoulder open and the other covered in clear crystals that were heavy at the top and tapered off toward the ruched waistline, Darcy didn't know if she'd ever seen a more beautiful dress.

"You made this?" she asked as she stared over at Victoria. "In two days?"

Laughing, Victoria nodded. "I did and I have to say, I think you'll look stunning in it."

Darcy's eyes locked onto the dress. Colin had

requested this for her? He'd not only requested it, he'd been specific about what he'd wanted.

Darcy swallowed, unable to even comprehend this world she was temporarily living in.

"Would you mind if I took Iris out for a walk?" Victoria asked. "Stefan and I were going to go down to the beach before the guests start arriving and things get crazy around here."

Still in a daze, Darcy turned back to Victoria. "Oh, sure. Of course."

Victoria lifted Iris into her arms and kissed her neck until the baby giggled. "Let's go get some sand between our toes."

"Thank you," Darcy said before Victoria cleared the doorway. "The dress is spectacular, so 'thank you' seems so inadequate."

Victoria nodded and grinned. "It was my pleasure. I'll bring Iris back shortly. You look like you could use some time to let all of this sink in."

Just as Victoria reached the doorway, she turned and glanced over her shoulder. "I know it isn't my place, but I can't let this go. Mikos left here because he couldn't face being a widowed father. Between all of the responsibilities and losing his wife, he was severely broken. He was only looking out for Iris when he left. She's always been his number one priority, so whatever he said or didn't say to you, was only to protect her in the long run."

Victoria slipped out the door, shutting it with a soft click. Iris's squeals could still be heard, but Darcy was stuck on Victoria's parting words.

A new plan started to form. Colin was coming for dinner and he expected her to wear the other blue dress.

What was it with him and blue? Apparently that was his favorite color.

She shook her head and focused on her plan. She'd wear the blue dress, but she was going to make him suffer. He might think he had control here, but they both knew she carried the power right now. She'd seen the vulnerability in him when she'd helped him up the steps and she'd seen how much he fought the weakness that continued to plague him.

But as far as their relationship went, she knew he still wanted her and most likely he'd planned dinner in her room as a way to seduce her. He may have started off lying to her, he may not have meant to hurt her, but he'd had ample opportunities to tell her the truth before taking her to bed.

If he wanted her for more than a romp, she wasn't going to give in so easily. She'd make him beg if she had to, because she was worth it.

Tonight she'd see what they both were made of.

Fifteen

Colin wanted to get to the room before the dinner arrived. He'd also asked Stefan and Victoria to keep Iris for a few hours this evening. He hated incorporating them into his plan, but he had to call for reinforcements because time was not on his side.

Taking a deep breath and willing his damn nerves to settle, Colin knocked on her door. He wanted time alone with Darcy, wanted to be able to let her into his life, his world because he'd come to realize she mattered more than he'd ever thought possible. At first the instant physical attraction had eaten at him, but he'd soon come to the conclusion that she was much more than someone he wanted to sleep with. Darcy was honest, invigorating and perfectly suited to him…someone he could spend the rest of his life with. The woman had woven her way into his world just when he wanted to be left alone the most. She'd awakened something fresh, something new inside of him he'd thought was long dead and gone.

When the knob turned and the door eased open, Colin's breath caught in his throat as his eyes traveled over the stunning image before him.

"I didn't think you'd actually wear it."

His eyes raked over the bright blue dress that wrapped over Darcy's breasts, dipping low enough for him to see the swell, then securing at her waist where her classy figure dipped in just above the flare of those hips that drove him insane with want and need.

She'd left her hair down, silky and straight. The barest of makeup made her seem so natural, so beautiful and so seamlessly matched to what he wanted but hadn't known he was looking for.

"Why wouldn't I?" she asked, gesturing for him to come on in. "You requested it. You are paying me, after all."

Cringing as he walked in, Colin hated that he'd thrown money in her face once again. He'd been so low as to dangle the very thing she needed and then relished his delight when he got his way.

He was no better than her ex and deserved nothing at all from the woman he'd found himself falling for.

Before he could say more, another knock sounded on the door and a member of the waitstaff rolled in a covered cart. He took it on out to the patio, bid them a good evening and was gone.

"Shall we?" she asked.

Not giving him a chance to answer, she headed toward the open doors that lead to the terrace. The ocean breeze slid through her room, bringing that familiar saltwater scent he'd taken for granted as a kid, but positively loved now. And he realized how much he'd missed the island now that he was back.

White table linens, gold candlesticks and a cluster of white roses adorned the table set for two. Darcy went to take the cover off of one of the dishes on the cart, but Colin stepped in front of her, blocking her action.

"You look beautiful," he told her, needing her

to know how he felt, that he believed what he was saying. "You're more than I deserve right now."

She tipped her chin, leveling his gaze. "I'm your nanny, Colin. Or would you prefer Mikos? Perhaps Your Highness. What do your other servants call you?"

"You're not my damn servant." Colin gritted his teeth. She was mocking him. "You can call me Mikos or Colin. Either would be fine."

She bowed and something in him snapped. He gripped her shoulders and gave her a slight shake.

"Don't bow to me. Ever."

Her eyes widened as she ran her tongue over her plump, glossy lips. "I'm your employee, am I not?"

"You're more, damn it, and you know it."

She stiffened beneath his touch. "Do I? Because I assumed even friends were up front with each other. Employees and employers keep their private lives separate, so excuse me if I'm a little confused."

He needed some space to cool off and she needed to get used to the fact that he wasn't going to give up so easily.

Releasing her, he pulled out a chair. "Sit. I'll get your dinner."

Surprisingly, she obliged. Once he'd served the meal, they ate in strained silence. Thoughts, possible conversations played over and over in his mind. There was so much he wanted to say, needed to say. But would she hear him, would the words penetrate into her heart where he needed them to go?

Pushing away from the table, Colin came to his feet and moved to the rail of the terrace. Watching the water ebb and flow against the shoreline calmed him. He absolutely loved his home, loved this view he was blessed to wake up to every day. It was all the hype around his name, his title that he could live without. He wanted a simple family life and the ability to live without the media snapping photos of him and his daughter, splashing whatever headlines they chose.

Stefan and Victoria had managed to attain such a life. They were making it work with their titles and they always managed to find time to themselves, away from all the hype and press. Could he have that, too? Could he attend to his duties and actually have a family?

His heart clenched. He hadn't known how much he wanted a family…a family with Darcy and Iris.

"I stared at this view for hours after I came home from the hospital," he started as he kept his back to her.

He hadn't counted on talking, but he couldn't keep her shut out of his world…not if he truly wanted her to be a part of it. And now more than ever he knew what he wanted.

"I'd sit out on the balcony off the master suite and curse that damn wheelchair. Karina was pregnant and all I could think was what type of father I could be to our child when I couldn't even stand or put on my own pants."

Darcy's chair scooted against the tile, but Colin kept his back to her. He couldn't turn and look her in the eye, didn't want to see pity staring back at him.

"I gradually got stronger, but I was too busy working on myself to realize I had to keep working on my marriage. Karina went through the pregnancy pretty much alone because I devoted all of my time to my recovery. I was determined to be on my feet when our baby came."

From the corner of his eye he saw Darcy step up to the rail, but far enough away that she was just out of reach. Probably for the best. With his emotional state, if she touched him, if she offered compassion right now, he'd break down, and baring his heart was about all the vulnerability he could handle. No way in hell did he want to be that man who clung to a woman, sobbing… which is exactly what he feared would happen if he didn't concentrate on the words and not the feelings of the past.

"When Iris came my whole outlook on life changed," he went on as he watched a palace guard pass by below. "The media wanted pictures of her, wanted photos of the happy family. It was then I realized we weren't a family. Karina had started sleeping in another room, she started distancing herself more and more from me and I can't blame her."

"It takes two to make a marriage work," Darcy added, her soft voice hitting him square in the heart. "You can't take all the blame."

Risking a glance over his shoulder, Colin met her intense gaze. No pity lingered in her eyes, if anything he saw understanding.

"I abandoned her long before she decided to leave," he replied. "After she suddenly passed away, I couldn't handle the strain of my life here any longer. It's no secret to my family that I've never wanted to be Prince of Galini Isle. I didn't want that weight on my shoulders. Stefan took the lead as king, which was fine with me, but if anything happens to him, I have no choice as long as I retain my title."

The familiar twinge in his back started out dull, the way it always did before blowing up into something major, so Colin pushed off the rail and stood straight, twisting at the waist to keep the muscles warm.

"Are you okay?" she asked.

"Fine. Just needed to move."

She stared at him another minute before looking back out to the water. "I have no clue about the life you were running from. I see this place and I think you have it all. But then I hear the pain in your voice and I know you are torn. I know you don't take this for granted and you're seriously worried about what step to take next."

Turning to fully face her, Colin took a step

closer. "I'm not only worried about the title, Darcy. I'm worried about us."

Shaking her head, her lids lowered as she bit her lip for a moment before speaking. "How can *us* even exist? There was one night. One amazing night, but it was built on lies."

He started forward again, but halted when she held out her hand. With a deep breath, she turned to face him. "You don't understand how deeply you hurt me. You can't imagine what it cost me to come to you that night. I kept avoiding you because you had everything I always thought I was looking for and I was terrified if I let my guard down, I would want too much. I would love too much."

Breath caught in Colin's throat. "Darcy—"

"No." She shifted, backing up a step as if she feared he'd reach for her. "Whatever I felt wasn't real because I developed feelings for a man who doesn't exist."

Swallowing hard, damning any risk he was about to take, he closed the distance between them and gripped her arms. She fell against his chest, her mouth opening in a gasp.

"Does this feel fake to you?" he demanded,

holding on to her a little too tightly. "Every time I kissed you, touched you, did all of that feel like a lie?"

Her intense gaze held his as he continued to loom over her. She'd cracked open something deep within him, something he hadn't even known he was holding back. His heart was wide open for her and she just needed to walk through. Damn it, he needed her to.

"You were so brave, calling me, wanting to come to me." He softened his voice. "You realized what we had was worth putting yourself out there for and you were ready to take a chance. Don't back away now, Darcy. Don't make judgment calls until you really see the big picture."

With the way he stood over her, her body arched against his, Colin couldn't avoid temptation another second. Nipping his lips against hers, testing to see if she'd let him continue, he nearly wept with relief when she didn't pull away.

As he wrapped his arms around her, pulling her hips flush against his own, he covered her mouth completely and deepened the kiss. Darcy's hands remained at her sides, though her mouth opened, inviting him in. For a split second, she froze, as if her mind were starting to override her emotions.

"No," he murmured against her lips. "Don't think. Feel. I never lied about how I feel and you know that. Everything we shared with our bodies was real. Everything I ever told you about how I felt was real."

With her eyes closed, she licked her swollen lips. "I can't do this, Colin. I'm here for Iris."

"Well I'm here for you," he whispered.

Not giving her another chance to speak, he claimed her mouth once again and ran his hands around to the front of her dress. He gave each side of the material a yank to expose her lace-covered breasts. On a gasp, Darcy tore her mouth from his and he feared he'd gone too far, but she tipped her head back and groaned. Colin stole the chance to trail a path of kisses down her silky skin until he reached the edge of the lace bra.

Darcy's hands fisted in his hair as he turned and backed her up against the smooth stone next to the patio doors. The last thing he wanted was to stay close to the rail and have one of the guards look up. Darcy was his and sharing even a glimpse of her was not an option.

Colin reached down, bunched up the bottom of her dress and slid his hand over her heated center. She adjusted her stance as he tore away her lacy panties and he had no doubt they matched the bra he was about to remove.

With a flick of his fingers, the front closure sprang open. Colin feasted on her while his hand continued to pleasure her. Her heavy panting quickened as her body arched against the stone. This is how he wanted Darcy, delirious with passion, aching with a need only he could provide because he was the only man for her.

"I pictured this the moment I saw the dress," he murmured against her heated skin. "It was made for you, made to drive me insane with wanting you."

Her hands went from his hair to his shoulders. Fingertips dug into him, but he continued, ready to feel her release, to watch her come apart in his arms.

As her hips bucked against him, Colin lifted his head to see her face. When he glanced up, her eyes were on him. The intensity of her gaze flooded him with a hope he wasn't sure she even knew she was offering.

Within seconds she was flying apart, calling his name. Colin gritted his teeth, concentrating on making this moment all about Darcy, no matter the cost.

As her trembling ceased, Colin slid his lips against hers. "You're mine for the ball tomorrow."

When she started to speak, Colin laid a finger against her lips. His other hand smoothed down her skirt as he kept his eyes on hers.

"Whatever you may think of me, know that I want you and I don't just mean physically. Yes, I lied. I did it to protect Iris because in the beginning she was all that mattered. But now you matter, too, more than you could ever know, and I'm giving you the chance to see everything about me without any guard on my heart. I want you to take it all in before you decide anything."

With shaky hands, she refastened her bra, pulled her dress back into place. "What about... you're not leaving now, are you?"

He smiled. "You mean why aren't we having sex? Is that what you want right now, Darcy?"

Her eyes held so much heat, so much desire. "I don't know what I want," she whispered. "I thought I did."

As much as it cost him, he took a step back. "I'm not staying and I'm not making love with you. Tonight was all about you. I wanted you in that blue dress because I knew you'd feel beautiful. I wanted you out here on the balcony for dinner because I know you normally eat fast to get back to taking care of children. And I wanted you to come apart in my arms without giving anything in return to me. From here on out, everything in my life will be centered around my daughter and you. Take all the time you need to think about what that means because I'm not going anywhere."

Her chin quivered. If she started crying, he'd have to hold her and he wasn't sure he was strong enough to wrap his arms around her and not take more than she was ready for at this point. Never in his life had he been this scared of losing it all. Even when he'd battled with his duties or being confined to a wheelchair, nothing had put fear in him as much as the thought of losing Darcy.

"Not all guys take everything, Darcy. Don't compare me with the jerk who shattered your dreams." He started toward the open French doors, but stopped at the threshold to look back at her. "I may just be the guy who can make your dreams come true if you'd take the time to look beyond the anger."

Oh, how he hoped she would do just that. Living without Darcy was simply a life that was unthinkable.

Sixteen

Colin swirled the amber liquid around in his glass, resisting the urge to throw it across the room. He hadn't heard a word from Darcy since leaving her room last night. The ball was in a few hours and he honestly had no idea if she was going to be there with him or not.

But right now he couldn't care less about the ball. He wanted to know where he stood with Darcy. He'd bared his soul to her, he'd passed all power over to her and now he had to wait. This was not how he lived his life…ever. Power and control were staples in his life, ingrained in him at a young age. But Darcy was worth giving all of that up for. She was worth every sacrifice.

"You're going to drive yourself mad and drinking won't help."

Colin didn't turn at the sound of his brother's useless advice. "If I want to drink, I will."

Standing on the balcony off his suite, Colin wasn't calmed by the water rushing the shore. For the first time in his life, he was consumed by emotions he had no control over: fear, frustration, worry.

"Luc just arrived." Stefan's shoes scuffed over the tile as he leaned against the rail beside Colin. "I told him you'd be down shortly."

Colin wanted to see his best friend, especially since he hadn't met Luc's fiancée yet. But he had to get his head on straight first. He couldn't go down to the ball with this much emotional baggage. Even if the media had not been permitted inside, he didn't want fellow dignitaries to see him so vulnerable.

"What have you decided?" Stefan asked.

Tilting back his glass, Colin welcomed the burn of the whiskey. "I haven't decided anything."

"Because of Darcy?"

Colin shifted, leaning one elbow on the rail as he stared at his brother. "You were a mess on your coronation day, if I recall. I know I was fresh from the hospital and in a wheelchair, but I remember how you were torn up over Victoria leaving you."

Stefan nodded. "She was my wife."

"Only because you needed her to be," Colin corrected. "You married her for one reason and fell in love with her later. It's no different with Darcy and me. She started out as Iris's nanny, but…"

Stefan's eyes widened. "Are you saying you're in love with her?"

Colin swallowed, afraid to say the words aloud. He merely nodded because the first time he admitted the truth verbally, it would be to Darcy, not his brother.

"And you're waiting to see what happens with you two before deciding whether to keep your title or not?"

Colin glanced out to the ocean, contemplating his next decision because no matter what he chose, the outcome would be life-altering.

"I'll remain on Galini Isle if Darcy stays with me." Colin pushed off the rail, began to pace in an attempt to release some tension. "I can't do this alone, Stefan. Raising Iris, helping you reign over this country. I won't leave Iris to be raised by staff, not when I have a woman I can't live without, and Iris loves her. I've realized that Iris is happy here or in LA but she is really attached to Darcy. And so am I."

Stefan smiled. "Then maybe you should tell her how you feel. I'm not the one you need to be selling this to."

Colin stopped in front of his brother. "You think she's a good fit for me?"

"I think Victoria is crazy about her and it's obvious Iris is, too." Stefan slapped a hand on Colin's shoulder. "And I've never seen you this torn up over a woman. I've also seen you face cliffs that would make even the most experienced climber cringe. Even after your accident you wanted to get back out there. You were angry the doctors wouldn't allow it. So the fact this woman has you in knots, yeah, I think she's a perfect fit."

"Then I need your help."

Colin laid out his plan, ready to fight for the woman he loved…the woman who completed his family.

* * *

The risk he was taking was huge, but the payoff would be substantial if every part of his plan fell into place.

Victoria had delivered Colin's message to Darcy that he wanted to meet her in the south hall, just outside the private entrance into the ballroom. Now he paced as Iris sat on the gleaming marble floor, playing with the simple doll Darcy had given her that first day.

He'd battled over whether or not to have Iris present for this moment; he didn't want Darcy to think he was using his child. But he needed Iris here because they were a package deal, they were a family.

The soft click of heels echoed behind him. Colin took in a deep breath, willed himself to be strong and prepared to fight for what he wanted.

"Deedee pitty!" Iris exclaimed before she jumped to her feet.

"You are beautiful." Darcy's upbeat voice gave him hope that she wasn't miserable, that she wasn't dreading tonight. "Your gold gown is so pretty, Iris. What a big girl you are tonight."

Pulling up a courage he'd never had to use before, Colin turned and was nearly brought to his knees. Darcy stared across the open space. She wore the gown he'd asked his sister-in-law to make, she'd pulled her hair back into something sleek and fit for a princess and she wore the diamond earrings that had been his mother's. Obviously Victoria had delivered those along with his message, but Colin hadn't expected her to wear them, though he was so glad she had.

Yet, as breathtaking as Darcy was right at this moment, it was the sight of her holding Iris's hand that stole his breath away. The two most important women in his life stared back at him, waiting for him to say something, but he was utterly speechless.

"Thank you for the dress." Darcy took a step forward, and Iris, still holding onto her hand moved with her. "I've never felt so...I don't know what the word is."

"Breathtaking," he murmured. "You're positively breathtaking."

Her eyes widened. "I could say the same for you. I've never seen you in something so formal."

The standard royal uniform of a black double-breasted jacket with gold buttons, his medals for

various works and services and his signature blue
sash meant nothing to him. His entire life on
Galini Isle meant nothing without this woman
by his side.

"Are you ready to go in?" she asked, smoothing her hand down her gown as if nerves were
getting to her, too.

"Not just yet. I wanted a minute alone with you
before we go inside."

Darcy glanced down at Iris before meeting his
gaze again. "I actually wanted to talk to you,
too."

No. He refused to hear her say she couldn't do
this anymore. He needed to tell her everything
he'd planned before she made any decisions.

"Let me start," he told her.

"Me, me, me." Iris let go of Darcy's hand and
extended both arms up. "Deedee hold me."

Laughing, Darcy swung Iris up into her arms.
Colin wanted to capture this mental picture of
Darcy in that pale blue gown and Darcy in her
gold dress with matching gold headband, both
of them laughing and smiling at each other. The
bond those two had formed had been instant.

Colin zeroed in on the doll Iris clutched. He'd

frowned upon it at first, but realized now how much it represented. Life could be simple, he could still have a normal existence, as long as Darcy shared it with him. Every relationship took work and he was ready to put forth every effort to make sure Darcy was in his life and happier than she'd ever been…if she would have him.

"Colin." Her eyes held his as she stepped forward. "What did you want to say?"

"I love you."

Darcy jerked, her gasp audible in the nearly empty hall.

He cursed beneath his breath. "That's not how I wanted to tell you. I wanted to lead into it by telling you how you've changed my life, how you've brought out something in me I thought was dead."

Colin closed the last bit of space between them, placing a hand on her arm and another on Iris's back. "I wanted to tell you how being without you all day has nearly killed me and how going to sleep at night without hearing your voice has left me feeling empty. I needed you to know how much you mean to me, how much you mean to

Iris before I told you how deeply I've fallen in love with you."

Unshed tears swam in Darcy's eyes. "You're going to make me ruin my makeup."

He gently swiped the moisture just beneath her lashes. "I want to be the man who ruins your makeup for all the right reasons. I want to bring tears of joy to your life, I want to lie by your side every night, knowing you're happy and that I've done everything in my power to give you all the love you deserve, all the happiness you can handle."

Darcy bit her lip and lowered her lids as Iris laid her head on Darcy's shoulder and cuddled in closer.

"I can't give you any more children," she whispered. "I know you'll want more heirs."

He shut her up with a soft kiss to her lips. "The only thing I want is you and Iris. You both will complete my family."

She glanced up at him, one tear trickling down her cheek. Colin swiped it away with the pad of his thumb and cupped the side of her face.

"We can adopt, too." He watched as her eyes widened, her breath hitched. "I'll adopt as many babies or children or teenagers as you want. I'm not above giving children a home. I love that you have such a strong will to help others and I know you'll make an amazing princess of Galini Isle."

"Colin," she whispered on a gasp. "What—"

"I want you to marry me."

Darcy wrapped her other arm around Iris and continued to hold his stare. Iris's eyes were slowly drifting closed, as this was her bedtime, but between the ball and Colin wanting her to be part of this monumental moment, he couldn't just leave her to sleep in her room.

"Have you thought about this?" she asked. "Have you thought about what having someone like me will do to the media you tried so hard to dodge so you could find the life you wanted?"

"I found the life I wanted," he told her, stroking her damp cheek. "I found you. I wasn't even sure what I was looking for, Darcy. I wanted to be alone, I wanted to figure things out, but you kept working your way deeper into my heart and I can't be without you now. No matter where we live, I want to be with you. Facing this country, standing by my brother's side is what I'm supposed to do. I just don't want to do it without you."

"I have a life in America, Colin. I have a business I'm trying to save because of a promise I made to my grandmother. I can't ignore who I am, I can't lose my identity."

Colin nodded. "I understand. You will restore Loving Hands to its former glory. I don't want you to lose your identity, either, because it's what made me fall in love with you to begin with. See what staff you can hire back and have someone manage the office while we are here. So much can be done online, but I'm assuming you have someone you'd trust to run the office?"

Darcy nodded, her eyes darting away as if she were already thinking through the plans that would need to be made.

"Tell me we can make this work," he pleaded. "We can even keep the home in LA to use when we go back."

"You'd come with me when I go to check in on Loving Hands?" she asked, her eyes wide, brimming anew with unshed tears.

Colin wrapped his arm around her waist, tucking her side against his so he didn't squeeze Iris too much now that she was sound asleep. So much for her taking part in his epic moment.

"I have to admit, I'm quite fond of those steps," he muttered against her mouth before he slid his lips across hers. "I think keeping that house is a great idea."

"I'm still under contract, you know. What happens at the end of my six-month term?"

"We can make it our wedding date, if you'll have me."

Darcy sighed into him, opening her mouth beneath his. Everything about her felt right, perfect. How did someone from a completely different world fit so effortlessly into his?

He eased back. "I should tell you, I allowed a trusted media source into the ballroom. If you agreed to stay with me, I wanted to be in control of who revealed our good news first."

She froze, her eyes searching his. "I thought you hated the media."

"I hate the stories they make up and how they were portraying Iris and me as broken. We're a strong force, and with you by our side we are even stronger."

Darcy smiled. "You're an amazing father. I love you, Colin."

He'd never tire of hearing those words. "What was it you wanted to talk to me about?"

Her smile widened. "I was going to tell you I wanted to give us another chance."

Shocked, Colin eased back. "You mean you let me go through all of that knowing you were giving me another chance?"

With a shrug, she shifted Iris a bit higher in her arms. "I wanted to know how far you'd go. I needed to see you grovel, just a bit."

Sliding a hand around her waist, Colin leaned in to whisper in her ear. "You want to see groveling? I still owe you a shopping trip and I plan on helping you in the dressing room. We'll see who's groveling then."

Before she could utter a word, Colin wrapped his arms around his girls and ushered them out. After putting Iris in her bed with a staff member close by the nursery, Colin whisked his future princess into her first royal ball. The first of many royal gatherings they'd be attending as a family.

* * * * *